The Cuckoo's Child

The Cuckoo's Child

by Suzanne Freeman

Greenwillow Books, New York

Library of Congress Cataloging-in-Publication Data
Freeman, Suzanne T.
The cuckoo's child / by Suzanne Freeman.
p.   cm.
Summary: Mia refuses to believe that
her parents are not coming back
after they're reported lost at sea.
ISBN 0-688-14290-7
[1. Separation anxiety—Fiction.
2. Parent and child—Fiction.]
I. Title.   PZ7.F8775Cu 1996
[Fic]—dc20
95-8385   CIP   AC

For Nannie and Duck

CHAPTER

1

The week after my parents vanished I tried to climb the water tower in Ionia, Tennessee. I hoped to see the ocean. It was a hot, windy day, and grit from the cement works pelted my face, making me blink. That morning my sister Bibi had teased my hair to cheer me up, and now, in the heat, I felt it prickled out all around my head like a thistle blossom. Usually it hung down, fine and flyaway and not a good color: beige, the shade of a grocery sack.

I had been eyeing the tower since we'd arrived in Ionia two days earlier, and finally, that afternoon, I decided to go up. I didn't tell my sisters when I left the house. They were supposed to take care of me while Kit, our aunt, was at work, but they spent all their time out in the porch swing eating cashews and reading novels in French to show off.

"Who wants to play crazy eights?" I'd asked, but they

wouldn't even look up. I knew they were just reading love stories, but their French books had plain paper covers that looked intellectual, and heavy, folded-over pages that my sisters sliced open, importantly, with butter knives from my aunt's kitchen.

"Want me to fix lunch?" I asked. "I can fix baloney sandwiches."

Bibi looked up, reluctantly, from her book. "None for me," she said. "I'm just going to have a coffee."

"Me, too," Nell said. She tapped her butter knife against the porch railing. *"Ennui."* She sighed. *"Tristesse."*

"We're back in America now," I said. "You can speak English."

The branches of two huge catalpa trees brushed across the porch roof, sounding like drum whisks. My sisters turned back to their books, slicing pages and pushing their bare feet against the floor to rock the porch swing, back and forth, back and forth. My palms itched. I couldn't wait around any longer.

"Maybe we should call the police," I suggested, "and see if they have any news for us."

My sisters didn't answer. I thought I could feel the weight of the hot, damp air, as if somebody were resting a hand on the top of my head. Over on the hillside the water tower gleamed, dully, against the hazy sky, the highest point in town. Suddenly I knew what I was going to do. What I had to do.

"You're making me nervous, just standing there, Mia." Nell spoke from behind her book. I stood there for another half a minute anyway, rooted to the scene. It changed things, having a plan. My sisters swung there idly, so unknowing. I already felt bad for them, for how they would worry when they noticed I was gone.

Up close, the water tower was much taller than it had appeared from Kit's house. When I leaned back to look up at the tank, its sides seemed to bulge, as if it were breathing. I hesitated. I knew I wasn't brave. But at least I was used to climbing. In Beirut, where we had been living, I shinnied to the top of the date palm trees on the playground almost every day and swayed there, hidden in the leaves, until one of my sisters was sent to tell me it was time to eat dinner or practice my music. Getting down from a palm tree was harder than climbing up, and I had scrapes all along the insides of my legs that I had to treat every night with Mercurochrome. Bibi told me if I kept it up, I would need a skin graft. But I wouldn't stop. From the tops of those trees, I could look across the street to the Mediterranean Sea and watch for any American ships that might be coming in. If no ships came, I would just beam messages, by mental telepathy, across the ocean, in the direction I hoped was toward the U.S.A. I spent most of my time being homesick. We had been living in Beirut for more than three years, and I was missing out on being an American kid.

I could name just what I was missing: sloppy joes and corn on the cob and going to watch *Dumbo* at the ten-cent matinees on Sundays. I wanted to drink school milk from the small waxy cartons printed with pictures of the presidents, and I wanted to sniff my hands for the strong, dull smell they gave off after catching lightning bugs. It was 1962, and I knew, from reading *Life* magazine, that there were new things I was missing, too: Barbie dolls, Caroline Kennedy riding her pony around the White House, teenagers dancing the twist. I kept magazine clippings in a scrapbook in my room, along with every letter I'd received from the friends I'd made in school where we used to live, in Ohio. They didn't tell me much— that it was snowing out or that school was as boring as ever—but I treasured them for the stationery with pictures of Little Lulu or Daisy Duck.

It wasn't that I hated Beirut. I liked the way it seemed pretty and dirty at the same time. The long flight of concrete stairs near our school always smelled as if somebody had just peed there, but small wild orchids grew out of the gaps in the concrete. I liked the tall white buildings and the tramcars and the beaches, where I collected sea sponges that rolled in on the foamy waves. I liked riding in the Cadillac taxis that went speeding along the Corniche with their tail fins bumping up and down. But I wanted to go home. Every morning, when I woke up, I tasted the Beirut air, tangy with salt and exhaust fumes and lemon blossoms, and I knew I wasn't where I was supposed to be.

It made me nervous that my dad was so happy teaching geology there, as if we might stay forever. From the balcony of our apartment he showed me how quickly the texture of the land changed from the seacoast to the slopes of Jabal Makhmal, where the cedar trees grew. He stooped down to my eye level and outlined the mountain range with his hands. I tried to pay attention. I had always loved my dad's looks, his coppery hair, his long, bony arms and legs, the sharp ridge of his nose. He looked as if he should be some kind of geological formation himself. But now I didn't want to think about bodies too closely. Jill Pillsworth, who was a grade ahead of me, had complicated everything, by always talking about IT. She seemed to know all the details.

"They breathe really hard when they do IT," she said, panting to demonstrate. "The whole bed shakes. God! Can you imagine your parents doing *that?*"

"Maybe your parents do," I said. "Not mine."

The Pillsworths lived in the apartment across the hall from us, and Jill and I walked together every morning to the American Community School while Bibi and Nell went in the other direction to the French school. On our way to school Jill tormented me by pretending to hitchhike whenever a diplomat's limousine came down the Corniche or wolf-whistling when we passed groups of Moslem women heading for the market, hidden in their long dark veils. Nothing fazed her, but everything mortified me. I wanted, more than anything, to walk to school in an American town where I looked like everybody else. I wanted to just blend in.

Some mornings, when I arrived at the Pillsworths', Jill opened the door and hissed, "IT! Last night. I heard them!" She nodded toward her parents, who sat at the table, eating toast and reading the paper. I stood there, blushing, while Jill ran around, collecting her books. I looked at the pattern on the red Turkish rug. I didn't want to picture anything. Mrs. Pillsworth worked in our school library. She had a kind, tired face that looked like Betty Crocker's picture on the cake mix. Mr. Pillsworth taught theology. He was known for his shiny, bald head and his habit of wearing bow ties. After standing there for a while, I relaxed. It didn't seem likely that anyone could just chew toast after spending the night doing the things Jill had described.

But when Mr. Pillsworth got up from the table and leaned down to kiss Mrs. Pillsworth good-bye, my face burned again. The dome of his head, bending down to hers, seemed so private. IT. Of course it was true. And, miserably, deep down, I wanted it to be true. It made my heart thump.

On the balcony my dad explained the world to me in terms of geology. He contrasted the formation of Beirut's mountain range with the small hills that had ringed our town in Ohio. He rounded his fingers to represent the hills.

"Now, I've told you all about the glaciers before."
I nodded.
"Okay. Then what word comes to mind here?"
I looked at his two cupped hands and looked away.

"Bosoms" was the word that came to my mind. I felt my face heat up. I shook my head unhappily.

"Mia," he said patiently, "moraines."

Almost halfway up the water tower now, I stopped to rest. I slid my legs through the rungs of the ladder and let my plaid sneakers dangle. I wondered if Bibi and Nell had missed me yet. I wished they would look up and recognize me, a small silhouette against the vast, hazy sky. Below me, Ionia was spread out, a mishmash of shingle roofs and tidy yards with browning grass and clumps of peony plants. This was my mom's hometown, although she never thought much of it. "I-oink-ia" she called it, because when she was growing up, all the outskirts were pig farms. Now, as far out as I could see, there were houses and church steeples and a narrow river threading along a reddish muddy bank. I thought of my mom as a young girl, whizzing down the cracked sidewalks here on her roller skates, leaping over the storm drains, turning cartwheels over the curbs. She was known for doing daring things. When she was seventeen, she eloped to Colorado and never went home again.

"I'm not having a normal childhood," I had complained to her, not long ago, in Beirut.

"Thank your lucky stars," she said.

I was in a gloomy mood that day because I had just come from a Girl Scout meeting where we held a party for two other girls in our troop whose families were moving back to the States. We gave them gold charms in the shape of cedar trees, and they cried. They had both lived in Beirut as long as they could remember. Now one was going to Washington, D.C., and one was going to Cincinnati. "Cincinnati!" I'd said to her. "The home of Tide detergent." She blinked at me with her wet pink eyes. I was fed up with American kids who didn't know how to be American. In school, when we said the pledge to the flag, it never came out right. Our voices didn't mix. We sounded like a chorus with everybody singing a separate, sad song.

"Mom," I said, "I mean it. I'm missing everything."

"Okay." She put down the nautical charts she had been studying and smoothed them in her lap. Her fingertips circled over the blue sea as if they were small boats, sailing every which way. My mother had been taking a course in navigation. Before, when we lived in Ohio, she took flying lessons. She came home with her eyes sparkling and told us about flying low over Lake Erie and seeing the shadow of the airplane move across the choppy gray water. We left for Beirut before she could get her pilot's license. Now she was planning a sailing trip that she and my dad were going to take off the coast of Greece. Every day she worked with her charts, plotting courses. Her gaze was distant, as if she were already scanning the horizon from the bow of a boat. "Okay," she said again. "What are you missing, exactly? What would make you happy?"

"Well," I said, "maybe a wiener roast."

My mom burst out laughing. The charts slid off her lap and swooped to the floor. "Come over here," she said, holding out her arms. But I hung back. It made me shy when she focused all her attention on me. "Come on," she said. I went over and sat on her lap. I felt too big, with my long, scarred legs covering hers, but I stayed there. I could hear the tick of her heart.

"A wiener roast," she said. "I think we can arrange that."

"Nah," I said. "It was just an idea." It was an idea I had taken from a series of books I'd been reading. They featured a gang of American brothers and sisters who solved mysteries, captured crooks, and foiled counterfeiters. In their free time they went on hayrides and had wiener roasts where somebody played the guitar by the campfire and everyone sang "Go Tell Aunt Rhody."

"Well, it's a good idea," Mom said. "In fact, it's just the kind of thing I'd like to do more of, eating outdoors, under the stars." She combed my hair with her fingers, smoothing it back from my face. "Thank you for thinking of it."

My bones seemed heavy, sinking onto hers. I never knew what to say when my mom believed the best of me and I didn't really deserve it. She was proud that I climbed the date palm trees every day, thinking that I did it from spunk or a spirit of adventure, instead of from despair.

"A wiener roast," she said. "Okay!"

The night before my parents left for Greece, we sat on the rocks by the sea, listening to motorboats speed across the dark water. Earlier we had roasted canned Danish hot dogs on sticks over a fire. When they sizzled, they made my mouth water, but when we wrapped them in Arabic bread and bit into them, they were rubbery. After we ate, a snorkeler came up from the edge of the rocks and dropped a baby octopus by our feet to see if we would buy it. My dad said no, but the snorkeler stayed around, watching Bibi and Nell. He had a mustache as thin as an eyebrow. He stood there smiling and cocking his head to get water out of his ear. After a while he picked up the octopus and threw it back into the sea. It left an oily patch on the rocks.

Dad poured water from his canteen into a pot to heat for coffee. "This is great," he said. "It feels as if we're camping out."

"It's getting buggy," Nell said. She lifted one ankle up and slapped at it delicately.

The snorkeler shifted around behind us. His flippers squeaked against the rocks.

"Mia, you look sleepy," Mom said. She blew me a kiss across the fire. Her bangs were crimped from the heat, and her freckles stood out against her pink skin. I remembered the story she used to tell about the night she left her first husband, Nell and Bibi's father. In her old white Plymouth she drove fast across empty roads in Colorado. She heard tree frogs making their lonely noise. She had nothing with her except some clothes and her two little daughters, asleep in the backseat. But every time the old car soared over a dip in the road, my mom could feel her heart lift. And every time she caught a glimpse of herself in the car mirror, as she moved farther and farther from her unhappy marriage, she could see the lines smooth out of her face. She looked younger and younger as she fled.

The water in the coffeepot began to sputter. Dad leaned over to lift it off the fire. "Here's something amazing to think about," he said. "All the water we drink is billions of years old. There's no such thing as new water."

I looked out over the Mediterranean. The moon had come up, off to the right, making a slanted path across the sea. "How about American water?" I said.

"All water, everywhere," Dad said. "The earth is a closed system. The exact same water is consumed and expelled again and again over the years."

"That's kind of disgusting," Nell said. "When you think about it."

"Au contraire," Bibi said. "I think it's kind of mystical."

The snorkeler began to sing, softly, in Arabic. When I turned around to frown at him, he blew a kiss at me, imitating my mom.

"What that means," Bibi said, "is that the water I drink might have been drunk before. By people who are dead now. Kings and queens. Saints."

"Criminals," Nell said. "Lepers."

The moon dazzled on the water. I was trying to be

happy, even though nothing was the way I'd hoped. In books the families didn't talk about dead people and drinking water. They talked about school and cheerleading and baking cookies. They visited grandparents on farms and learned to milk a cow. They were never complicated with first marriages or half sisters or mothers who flew. I blinked, trying not to cry. When I looked around again, at least the snorkeler had gone.

"Here." My dad handed my mom a cup of coffee. "Drink this and become a part of history."

My mom gestured out to the sea. "Tomorrow that's where we're going to be," she said happily. "Somewhere past the path of that moon."

"I want to go home," I said. My parents looked over at me and smiled.

"Somebody's tired," Mom said. "It's been a big day."

"Au contraire," I said. "It's been a little day. *Beaucoup petite.*"

"Uh-oh," Bibi said. "We know we're in trouble when she starts speaking fractured French."

"Au contraire, merde-brain," I said.

"So much for the family wiener roast," Nell said.

I started to cry. Mom came over and put her arms around me. "Ssh," she whispered. She smelled like smoke and Arpège.

"I just want to go home," I told her. She thought I meant our apartment in Beirut.

"That's where I'm taking you," she said. "Home."

*　*　*

Now, sitting halfway up the ladder, I began to doubt my mission on the water tower. When I peered through the rungs, the only faraway sight of interest was the cement works, carved out of the landscape in a rough circle. Mica chips twinkled in the huge heaps of sand. A machine droned somewhere in the background. I had no real sense of geography, but suddenly, plain sense told me that no matter how high I climbed there would be no ocean to see. A mud dauber buzzed close to me and then veered off, gone in the haze. I sat, rigid. My parents' boat was missing in the Ionian Sea, and here I was in Ionia, Tennessee. There should be a connection somewhere. I closed my eyes. If I touched my eyelids with my fingers, I saw red spots, like poppies, and I remembered a field on the campus in Beirut where scarlet poppies grew so thick that the wind left rippled lines across the surface, just the way fingers make streaks on velvet.

"Hey!"

I opened my eyes. A man had shouted from somewhere below. I didn't look down.

"You! Little girl. You're trespassing up there."

I stared straight ahead. I was probably going to get arrested. My bottom ached from balancing on the thin metal rung.

"Come on down. Now."

My hands were damp. I wiped them on my shorts so I wouldn't get bad blisters. I shifted sideways and eased my legs out through the ladder. Glancing down, I saw a dusty pickup truck with hay bales and orange traffic cones stacked in the back. A man wearing gray overalls stood just off to the side, his head tipped back, both hands framing his forehead like a visor. I didn't want to go down, but I couldn't think what else to do. In Beirut once I was chased by a security guard because Jill Pillsworth stole a handful of all-day suckers from a hotel gift shop. I had been standing there, reading the little verses in all the American birthday cards, when she shrieked, "Move it!" I ran, panicked, not knowing why, flinging a card behind me. Our feet stung from smacking the pavement, and the security guard chased us for more than a block before we ducked through the railings of an iron fence and lost him. The suckers were a kind of barley sugar made in Lebanon. We didn't like the taste, but sometimes they came with a prize: a twenty-five-piastre coin, taped inside the wrapper. On the playground outside our apartment building Jill and I tore all the wrappers off. There were nine suckers and not a single coin. "What a gyp," Jill said.

We smashed the candy against the poles of the swing set, and it splintered into bright shards that Jill said looked like the inside of a kaleidoscope and I said looked like broken church windows.

"Church!" Jill said. "Hoo-boy. You must have a guilty conscience."

And I did. For days afterward I wouldn't go near the swing set, but I also couldn't get out of my mind what it was like to be chased: the thud of our feet on the sidewalk and the guard so close behind us that we could hear his gun holster slap against his thigh. But most of all, I remembered how when we had made our getaway and stopped to rest, we breathed so hard our throats rasped, and it made us laugh and laugh, giddy with our luck.

This time, though, I didn't see how there would be any getaway, not with this overalls man and his pickup truck waiting at the bottom of the tower. I backed slowly down the ladder, trying to figure out a plan. I wondered if my mother had ever climbed this tower and what she would have done now. But it was too hard to guess. She was an adventurer, and I was not. When she had looked out over this view, it made her want to pack her bags, but I had looked out over the ocean again and again, wanting just this: the plain houses with TV aerials strapped to their sooty chimneys, the birdbaths twined with ivy, the heat vapors rising off the dull tar roads. I had made a crybaby's wish, and here it was, come true.

"Let's go," Mr. Overalls called. I was down close enough now to see the stiff comb marks in his hair. It looked polished, like a wicker basket. I stopped where I was. This was my last chance, up here, to do what I had come to do, to beam out a new message, even if I could not find the sea. I wasn't even as high as the treetops now, but I thought it might work if I focused on the sky. I could imagine a message ricocheting through space, bouncing off the stars, somehow.

"Hey," the man called, "climb on down now."

I looked up at the sky, and heat spread across my face. *Come back*, I beamed, with all my concentration.

"Okay, then," Mr. Overalls yelled. "I'm going to have to come up there after you. Is that what you want?"

Come back.

The ladder vibrated beneath me. Two birds, chasing each other, swooped low overhead. A car door slammed, echoing on the hillside.

Come back, and I promise I'll never complain about Beirut again.

"Mia! Hey, Mia!" I heard familiar voices, and when I looked down, I saw my mother, rushing toward me, calling my name. "Mom!" I said, but then I realized it was Kit. She ran just the way my mom did, with her elbows cocked back and her face knotted with effort. She was my mom's sister, but I hadn't met her before we came to Tennessee. I didn't want her looking like my mom now, like an imitation. I wanted her to go away.

Bibi and then Nell came struggling up the hillside now, following Kit, their sandals tripping them up as they tried to run.

"Mia!" Bibi called. "Get down from there!"

"It's okay," the man yelled down to them. "I've just about got her."

I wanted them all to leave me alone. I wanted my mom and my dad, only my mom and my dad. Mr. Overalls was getting closer. I felt the ladder jolt. That's when I knew what I needed to do: jump!

A hot breeze came sweeping across the ladder, stinging my legs with grit.

"Ouch," Mr. Overalls muttered, just below me.

If I jump, you'll come back.

"All right now," Mr. Overalls said. I felt his hand graze my ankles. "Take it easy and we'll get you down from here."

I jumped.

As I dropped, I didn't see my whole life pass before my eyes, the way everybody always says you will. I smelled the hard earth below me, nothing like the sea, and I felt the thick air lift my teased hair, in two broad flaps like Dumbo's ears.

2

"I'll tell you what you looked like," Bibi said. "A human sacrifice." She shuffled the cards and let them fall between her fingers.

"Yeah," Nell said. "You looked like you were having a religious experience, Mia. Like this." She rolled her eyes skyward and touched her palms together, like somebody praying.

"My hands weren't like that!" I protested, but I didn't mind. This was what I had always known it could be like, having sisters, talking and joking together. Ever since I'd come back from the hospital earlier in the morning, they had waited on me, bringing me root beer and Ritz crackers spread with pimiento cheese. I was wearing Nell's pink fleece bathrobe, and Bibi had promised that she would give me an egg yolk facial later on.

Now we were in Kit's living room, getting ready to

play cards. Bibi shuffled again. When I bounced on the sofa, dust motes flew up from the cushions and spun around in the dim sunlight. I loved the secret, personal smell of the dust, like sniffing somebody's hairbrush. I loved my sisters, facing me across the card table with their whitish pink lipstick and plucked eyebrows. I wanted to be just like them.

"Can I have a cigarette?" I said. *"S'il vous plaît."*

They looked at me. Nell exhaled a blast of smoke from her Lucky Strike that made her nostrils flare. "Are you nuts?" she said. "You just got out of the hospital."

"For observation," I said. "For a concussion. Big deal."

"Forget it, Mia," Bibi said. "You're too young. You're not going to smoke. Period." She tamped the cards on the table. "Okay. If we're playing old maid, I take three queens out of the deck and just leave the queen of hearts, right?"

"Right," Nell said. "And for your information, Mia, a concussion means a bruised brain." In Beirut Nell had spent her afternoons reading medical textbooks in the university library because she said she was going to be a surgeon someday and work for Albert Schweitzer in Africa. At dinner, night after night, she brought up topics from her reading, like dysentery and loa loa worms. It drove me crazy the way my parents listened to her attentively and asked her questions as if they took her seriously. I thought of her room, littered with Lucky Strike wrappers and hair spray cans, and it didn't seem like the room a future surgeon would have. Also, she couldn't sew. When she had to stitch the elastic straps into her ballet slippers, she gripped the needle with her teeth and tugged it through the fabric so she wouldn't chip a fingernail.

"You have to take it seriously whenever there is any trauma to the brain," Nell continued now. "Sometimes there are complications."

"Like what?" Bibi stopped sorting through the cards and looked up.

Nell rolled her eyes in my direction. "I think we should discuss that later," she whispered.

"Oh. Right," Bibi said. They both looked at me across the table and smiled.

"Can we just play cards?" I said. But now my heart wasn't in it. Watching them exchange looks and smile their superior smiles, I knew I'd been stupid to think they were including me when they were really just humoring me. The stories they'd told me this morning—about French school and leg waxing and sailors from the Sixth Fleet—probably weren't anything like the real stories they would tell later, after I was in bed. Then they'd sit up together, whispering and joking and blowing smoke rings. They'd always be real sisters and I would be the half sister.

I felt the same sharp pang of loneliness that I used to get when I stared out at the wide sea from my hiding place between the palm fronds. I sighed and picked up the cards that Bibi had dealt me. There was the old maid with her pale, snooty face.

"You can go first, Mia," Bibi said.

"For your information, I don't want to go first." I fanned my cards out and stared at them sourly.

"Oh, boy," Nell said. "Three guesses who has the old maid."

"Yeah," Bibi said. "You're subtle, Mia."

I shrugged. I took a Ritz cracker from the plate on the table and shoved it, whole, into my mouth. The telephone rang in the kitchen.

"I'll get it." Bibi arranged her cards facedown on the table and went out through the dark back hallway that led into the kitchen.

"I'll bet it's another neighbor calling to find out how Kit is doing," Nell said. "It's amazing how quickly the word gets around in a town like this." She took a deep draw on her cigarette and then let the smoke out slowly, shaking her head. "And you know what everybody's thinking: Poor old Kit! First, three nieces she's hardly ever seen arrive on her doorstep for an indeterminate stay. Next, one of those nieces jumps off the water tower and lands smack on top of her so she winds up hospitalized with multiple fractures."

"I don't think I landed on *top* of her." I swallowed the last of my cracker. "Anyway, she shouldn't have tried to catch me." I had no clear memory of the collision with my aunt, except for the shock of the impact and a faraway noise that had made me think of dried kelp crackling under my feet on the beach. Now it crossed my mind that it could have been the sound of breaking bones.

"Nell." Bibi's voice came from the end of the dark hallway. "Come here for a minute, would you?"

Nell scooted her chair back from the card table and stood up. "Honor system, Mia," she said. "No fair trying to ditch the old maid while we're out of the room."

I settled back into the sofa cushions to wait. I could hear the catalpa trees brushing the house and the moving branches made the sunlight dance around on the opposite wall. This house used to belong to my grandmother, but it was not the house where my mom grew up. Kit and my grandmother had moved in here after my grandfather died and my mother was already married and living in Colorado. It was a solid, boxy house with shiny reddish wood floors and curlicued metal heating grates. I liked the faded pastel paint on the walls—blue bathrooms, yellow kitchen, mint green living room—and I was glad to know that this was not the house my mom had decided to run away from when she was seventeen.

"It wasn't any one thing," Mom had said. "It was just a plain house with flowered curtains in the windows, like everybody else had. But you see, honey, I never wanted to have just what everybody else had."

She didn't elope by climbing down a ladder in the middle of the night but by packing her suitcase and walking out the front door early one April morning when the rest of her family was in the kitchen at the back of the house getting ready to eat biscuits and boiled eggs.

"That's what we always had, every Monday breakfast

of my life," she told me. "And when I climbed into the car and we drove off, past the high school where I had two months to go before graduating, onto the highway heading east, the sun just coming up in front of our eyes, I knew life never had to be like that again: biscuits on Mondays, oatmeal on Tuesdays."

The part I didn't like in this story was when my mom said "we" and I had to picture her, silhouetted against the sunrise, not with my dad but with somebody else, a soldier with wavy brown hair and a long jaw and the unromantic name of Morse Cooper. I had seen snapshots of Morse Cooper in Bibi and Nell's room, but I had never met him, and I didn't want to. He was like a shadow, hovering over our real family but not fitting in. There was no place for him.

I picked up the cigarette pack that Nell had left on the table and looked at the red letters printed on the bottom, *L.S.M.F.T.* On commercials they told you it stood for "Lucky Strike Means Fine Tobacco," but Jill Pillsworth had told me another version: "Loose Strap Means Floppy Tit." My head was starting to throb. In the other room my sisters murmured together. Suddenly I felt all alone. I missed Jill Pillsworth, her knowing laugh, the familiar mocking slant of her mouth when she teased me. She was my best friend. I started to cry, and it was the deep, messy kind of crying that feels like a relief. My chest shook. I had to wipe my nose with the wide, soft cuff of Nell's bathrobe.

Behind me, out in the front hall, the screen door slapped shut. "Yoo-hoo," a voice called. I sank lower into my chair. I wasn't ready to quit crying.

"Yoo-hoo," I heard again. A small gray-haired woman stepped into the living room. She was wearing orange potholder mitts on both her hands and carrying a glass casserole dish. She stopped when she saw me hunched down in the chair, my face all wet.

"Bless your heart," she said. She walked over and set the casserole down on the card table in front of me. It smelled good, like cooked onions. "I brought you-all some ham with scalloped potatoes," she said. "I'm Mrs. Swope, honey. I live over yonder, the green house across the road."

I knew I was supposed to answer something, but I kept on crying, without making any noise. My mouth cupped in. My eyes burned from the tears.

"Let me find you a hankie," Mrs. Swope said. "I came at a bad time."

I shook my head. Mrs. Swope stood there looking at me with concern. Her orange mitts were startling on her tiny arms, like boxing gloves on a kangaroo. I tried to take a slow, calming breath, but it came out ragged. "I have a bruised brain," I said finally.

"My nephew had that one time," Mrs. Swope said. "Way back when. Now he's all grown up, and he works for the county."

In the kitchen the telephone gave an abbreviated jingle,

which meant it had just been hung up. Bibi and Nell stayed there, talking together in hushed voices.

"Conway"—Mrs. Swope continued—"my brother's boy. It happened when he cracked his head on a stanchion."

My sisters were arguing about something now. From the other room their whispering sounded sharp, like a flag snapping in the wind. I watched steam rise up, fogging the glass lid of the casserole dish. "Well," Mrs. Swope said. She took a step toward the door, but I didn't want her to go yet. I didn't want to be by myself. I heard the clock on the mantelpiece, and the ticking seemed too fast.

"We can't find my mom and my dad," I blurted. "They're lost at sea."

Mrs. Swope stepped back toward me. "Oh, honey, I know," she said. "And I know what you're going through. My brother and I were orphaned at an early age and raised by our second cousin. Oh, my heart goes out to you-all."

Orphan! I looked at Mrs. Swope again. I had only read about orphans in books, and now here was one standing next to me. Mrs. Swope had thin, stooped shoulders, and I thought of Sara Crewe, starved and forced to carry heavy buckets of wash water to scrub floors. "That was nice of you," I said, "to make us a casserole."

"Oh, well." Mrs. Swope waved one orange mitt. "It isn't much. It's just the way we do down here, helping out."

My sisters came in from the kitchen. Nell had her glasses pushed up on top of her head. Bibi was eating a triangle of leftover toast, and she popped the last corner into her mouth so she could hold out her hand to Mrs. Swope. "I'm Bibi Cooper," she said. "And this is my sister Nell."

"May Swope," Mrs. Swope said, "from across the road." She had pulled off a potholder to shake my sisters' hands, and her fingers looked like little twigs, ready to snap.

"Mrs. Swope is an orphan," I told my sisters.

"Well," Mrs. Swope said, "I used to be."

The telephone rang again. My sisters looked at each other.

"He's calling back," Nell said. "About the tickets."

"Who?" I said. "Tickets for what?"

"I'll get it," Bibi said. She hurried from the room.

"Write everything down!" Nell called after her.

"Somebody my age can't still be thought of as an orphan!" Mrs. Swope chuckled and shook her head. "I'm old as the hills."

"What's going on?" I demanded. "Who is that on the phone?"

Nell pushed her glasses back down onto her nose and peered at me. "We can talk about it later, can't we, Mia? We have company now."

"I have to run along anyhow," Mrs. Swope said. "I just stopped by to leave this casserole with you-all."

"A casserole!" Nell said. "How wonderful. Wouldn't

you like to sit down, Mrs. Swope? Could I get you a glass of ice tea?"

"Well." Mrs. Swope's eyes darted back and forth from Nell to me.

"If you won't tell me, then I'll just go into the kitchen and listen." I rose from my chair, and instantly I felt dizzy. The long bathrobe was tangled around my legs. I stood there, rocking back and forth.

"Okay, okay!" Nell rushed over and put one hand on my shoulder. "Sit down, Mia. I'll tell you. It's no big deal anyhow."

But it seemed important to stay standing up. I clutched an edge of the card table. Nell patted my shoulder. She shook her head at Mrs. Swope. "Mia was just released from the hospital this morning. A concussion."

"Bless her heart."

I reached up and brushed Nell's hand off my shoulder. "Tell me right now."

"I wish you'd just sit down first."

"Tell me!"

Nell sighed. She looked at Mrs. Swope and shrugged. "It's my father on the phone." She reached down to the card table and straightened the fan-shaped group of cards that were lying facedown in front of her. "He wants Bibi and me to fly up there and visit him for a little while. In Boston, where he lives now."

I stood there. All I could do was watch Nell's hands, forming the cards into a more perfect fan. There was a picture of a waterfall on the back of each card, and everywhere I looked, I saw churning water, stopped in midair. Morse Cooper. He was still there, still worming his way into our life. I considered tipping the card table and watching everything slide off, cards, cracker plate, even the steaming ham casserole.

"Of course, we won't be going until Kit comes home from the hospital."

"That poor thing!" Mrs. Swope said. "I guess she broke both her arms."

"Hairline fractures of the radius." Nell assumed her clinical voice. "Also a cracked clavicle and numerous contusions."

"Oh, my."

"They're keeping her awhile longer because traction was indicated."

"My minister's wife had to have lumbar traction and wear some kind of brace."

"Yes, well, that's really a whole different process."

"She told me the pain was like a hot poker on her insides."

"Don't go, Nell." My voice croaked because my throat had gone dry. It felt as if someone else had spoken. It felt as if the words had hit the air and hung there, like words in a comic strip.

Nell and Mrs. Swope looked at me. I saw their blank faces.

"I mean it!" My voice came back. "You can't go off and leave me here."

"Her color doesn't look too good," Mrs. Swope said.

Nell stepped forward and put her hand on my shoulder again. "You need to sit down, Mia. You should rest your head between your knees. Right now. Come on."

My hands were curled under the rim of the card table, and it was easy to tip. It felt light. The casserole dish skidded over the edge and hit the rug fast, but the cards flew into the air and rained down as if all those tiny stuck waterfalls were in motion again. I took a deep breath.

"Mia! For God's sake!" Nell jumped around and tried to scoop things up. There was sauce from the casserole splattered on her feet. I stepped around the metal table legs and headed for my bedroom, behind the kitchen. Bibi was standing by the stove, still on the telephone. "What happened?" she mouthed when she saw me. I shrugged. I felt calm now and deeply sleepy, as if I'd just hiked over a mountain.

In my room I lay down on top of the corduroy bedspread. I smelled its dusty cotton smell. When I woke up, it was evening. The sun was gone from the back of the house, and the knotty pine paneling in my room made sharp, cracking sounds as it cooled off. This was the spare room, and it was filled with odds and ends: old radios, sewing baskets, and stacks of road maps from the company where Kit worked. She was a commercial artist for a road map publisher. I wasn't sure exactly what that meant. I didn't know anything much about Kit except that she was five years younger than my mom and she had a similar pattern of freckles sprinkled across her face. In high school she had been a basketball star. Her trophies were on a shelf in the back of the closet. Ever since we'd arrived in Ionia, she'd hovered around us, trying to make us feel better, and now it seemed as if everybody wanted me to be grateful because she'd jumped toward the water tower, arms outstretched, to catch me, like some rebound.

I turned over and traced a finger along the pine, wondering what kind of picture would appear if I could draw lines to connect the knots. There was a knock on my door, and Bibi came in.

"Mia?" She was holding a towel and a bowl. "I promised I'd give you a facial, remember?" She walked over to the bed and showed me the egg yolks, beaten to a golden paste. "You really slept, I guess. Your face has ridges from the corduroy."

She sat down and smoothed my hair away from my face. "Just so you know," she said, "Mrs. Swope's casserole dish didn't break. Not even a chip, luckily. But God, what a mess to clean out of the rug." She began to spread the egg goo over my cheeks and across the bridge of my nose, making circular motions with two fingers.

"Bibi."

"Ssh. You can't talk or this stuff will crack. It hardens fast."

"I don't want you to go."

She sighed. "I know. But, Mia, Nell and I haven't seen our father for more than a year. We just need to go right now. Can you understand that?"

"Don't leave me here with just *her*."

"Oh, Mia." Bibi wiped the egg off her fingers with a

paper towel. "Give her a chance. She's trying. She's never had kids around before."

I got up and switched on the lamp on my bureau. The egg yolk was a brittle yellow crust, and in the mirror my eyes were two dark craters, like an example in one of my dad's geology books. I thought of my dad's voice, of all the words he had told me: *esker, drumlin, paleozoic.* I had no idea what they meant. Oh, why hadn't I ever listened? How would I ever know anything now?

"Bibi," I said. "Oh, Bibi, where could they be?"

She came over and put her arms around me. "I don't know," she whispered. I saw in her eyes then, she was as scared as I was. "But it will be okay. Don't you think so, Mia? Don't you think everything will be okay?"

I nodded, acting brave, but my face crumpled, and the whole egg mask came apart, shattered.

CHAPTER

3

In the mail, two days later, I got my report card, forwarded by Mrs. Pillsworth, from Beirut. I was promoted and assigned to Mrs. Weill's class. Mrs. Weill was from Switzerland. She spoke with a German accent, and she wore her hair in a pixie cut that let her ears poke through in two pink crescents. I tossed the report card down and stretched out on the porch swing. I liked to stare up at the lacy pattern of dead moths in the lamp overhead as I rocked, sideways, in the swing. Sometimes the pattern looked like the outline of a stagecoach, and sometimes it was the profile of President Kennedy with his handsome cupped chin.

It had rained in the night, but now the sun was out, and you could also see a faint slice of moon low in the sky. The steamy air pressed on my skin, making me edgy. I wished I had a bicycle to ride or even a basketball to dribble down the street, now that my head was better. I had been in America for almost a week and I hadn't done any American things. The only places I had been were the water tower and the hospital. Kit owned a television, a big console set, but it was broken. It sat, heaped with papers and a candy dish full of linty sour balls, in a corner of the living room. I had plugged it in and switched it on once, just to check, and I thought I heard Walter Cronkite's voice, far away behind a loud eggbeater noise. Tubes lit up in the back of the set, and there was a sharp smell of plastic and hot dust, but nothing showed up on the screen.

I pushed my hand against the floor of the porch to make the swing move faster. Two sparrows landed on the telephone wire next to the house, and they were plain, dingy brown, just like any sparrows I could have seen from our balcony in Beirut. I picked up the report card and looked again at the typed words "Room Seven, Mrs. Weill." I got the message. As soon as my parents found their way out of the Ionian Sea, I would be right back in Beirut, swaying in the palm fronds as if nothing had ever happened. I'd spend my school year listening to Mrs. Weill's Katzenjammer voice and smelling the peculiar, foreign odor of our school's gloomy front hallway. It was spicy and dank at the same time, and it always made me think of cooked eggplant.

The two birds flew away suddenly, leaving the wire bouncing. I needed somewhere to go, something to do, before it was too late, before I was sent back. I didn't even know for sure what Ionia had to offer, but I guessed there would be a Woolworth's with hamsters and goldfish and warm Spanish peanuts, sweet underneath their papery skins; a Rexall store with a soda fountain and swiveling stools; a miniature golf course; and maybe a town swimming pool with a high diving board.

The screen door opened, and Nell came out, holding her French novel. Her hair was twisted into snail curls, crisscrossed with silver clips all over her head. "Shove over," she said. "You can't hog the whole swing."

I moved my feet, and she sat down, immediately opening her book and starting to read, squinting with concentration. The scent of Dippity-Do wafted from her head in the still, hot air. The dull swaying of the swing made me itch. I crossed my arms and scratched both shoulders hard.

"I just need to *go* somewhere," I said loudly. "*Do* something!"

Nell looked up briefly. "Don't claw yourself like that, Mia. You could get blood poisoning."

Overhead President Kennedy shifted his expression as the swing moved. Angry. Surprised. Angry. Surprised. In most of the *Life* magazine photos I'd seen he was smiling. He looked windblown and happy, walking on a beach or stepping off an airplane but, always, tired around the eyes. He had too many worries, mostly having to do with the Communists, who, Jill Pillsworth informed me, had missiles aimed, ready to strike every house in America.

"See, that's why we're safer here," she'd said. "We're lucky to be in Beirut."

I looked out the window of Jill's apartment, and I felt sorry for her. Her parents had moved here when she was a baby, and now this is what she thought home was: the tilted trees, the prayer sirens wailing, a concierge wearing a battered red fez.

"See, you don't really remember," I said gently. "I mean, it's not your fault. You're almost hardly even American."

"Is that so." Jill spoke each word separately, in a dangerously quiet voice. I felt my heart tick. She had power over me.

"Well, I mean, you *are* an American. I know that. I just . . ." My voice trailed away.

"Ummhmm. Well." Jill buffed her chewed-off fingernails idly on her shirt sleeve. She was taking her time, torturing me. "So," she said finally, "let's see now, who has the most American record albums?"

"You do."

"Hmmm." She blew on her fingertips and buffed them again. "And who has shaken hands with Art Linkletter?"

"You have."

"And"—she looked up now, with a pleased, malicious smile—"who has a *normal* American passport?"

There it was then. She knew all my weak points because I confided them to her, and she stored them up to use against me. My passport mortified me because on the blank where you could state your religious preference if you chose to, my mom had written "Unfettered!" and there it was in bold print anytime you looked inside the cover.

"You could have written 'unaffiliated,'" my dad suggested to her, "or even left it blank."

"I wanted to make my point," my mother said. "I refuse to have us be so easily labeled."

But I longed for those labels. I just wanted to say what I was—Methodist, Jewish, Lutheran—the way other kids did. On the rare occasions when my family went to any church, mostly on big holidays in Ohio, my mom just shopped around, reading the religious listings in the newspaper.

"Maybe the Service of Lessons and Carols at St. Augustine's," she'd say. "No. Wait. I can't resist this: The Living Messiah at Boulevard Baptist." One time she took us to a Negro church and we were the only white family there. People turned to watch us as we filed down the aisle, looking for seats, and I felt my face flame. My mom was bareheaded, and every other grown woman was wearing a hat. I pantomimed across Bibi and Nell, down the pew, to my mom, trying to make her understand. I patted the top of my head and lifted my eyebrows. She nodded and reached up to smooth her hair along its part. She fluffed her bangs with her fingertips and smiled at me. "Okay?" she mouthed.

Later, when I asked her why we went to so many churches instead of just one, she said, "For the richness. The variety. The *poetry* of all those liturgies." She was fixing sandwiches for lunch, and she waved the mayonnaise spoon at me for emphasis. "You know, sweetie, the Bible is the basis for every story in the world, and I think it's wonderful—fascinating!—to see how it's played out in different churches, don't you?"

"But what can I say when somebody asks me if I'm Lutheran or Unitarian or what?"

"The Unitarians!" Mom said. "Now that's a church we haven't been to for ages, and they really do interest me, their whole concept of what the Trinity is. Or isn't, I should say."

"So, could I say I'm a Unitarian then?"

"No." A dab of mayonnaise flew off the spoon and hit the countertop. "Sweetie, I don't think you're listening to what I'm saying. It's good to be different sometimes. It's interesting to be a person who cannot easily be labeled." She looked at my face. "Oh, okay, if you have to say something, just say you're a sophist." She scooped the mayonnaise from the countertop with the tip of her finger and licked it off. "No, I've got it. Even better, say you're an aesthete. A-E-S-T-H-E-T-E. That means a pursuer of beauty. That's what we are. A family of aesthetes."

But that was no help at all. An impossible, unpronounceable word that didn't name any regular church was not going to get me anywhere with Jill Pillsworth or any other kids. I couldn't even try it.

Most of the time I didn't believe half of what Jill told me, but sometimes, when I was at the top of a palm tree and I heard the drone of engines overhead, I'd panic, expecting to see a formation of missiles, like flying lipstick tubes passing over on the way to wipe out my country, to blow up everything I ever wanted. And being there, thousands of miles away, unharmed, in a tree only made me feel worse, left out again.

But now here I was on a porch swing in Ionia, Tennessee, and anything that happened to every American in every house would happen to me, too. I cheered up.

Nell put her book down in her lap and reached up to test her curls. She removed one pair of clips and a spiral of honey-colored hair dropped down to her shoulder. I would have given anything for hair like hers or even like Bibi's, which was a little darker but had gold streaks. "Still too wet," Nell said. She held the clips in her teeth as she wound the curl back up around her finger.

"How come you set your hair anyway?"

She shrugged. "Maintaining the standards, I guess." She let out a deep sigh. "Though, really, God knows why, in this little backwater."

"What's a backwater?"

Nell swept her arm out in a circle. "What you see all around you," she said. "A place where you can't buy a copy of *Vogue*, much less *Le Figaro*. A place where people's idea of *glace* is something from the Dairy-Freez. On a cake cone." She shuddered. "Like cardboard."

"This is America," I said. "Why should they have French magazines?"

Nell laughed. "There's America and there's America," she said, "as you will learn."

But I thought she was wrong. There was one big America, and what I loved about it the most was that it was all the same. That's how I knew that I would find Woolworth's and miniature golf somewhere nearby and that when I convinced Kit to get the TV repaired, I could count on watching "My Little Margie" and "Ramar of the Jungle." Now I also knew that there was a Dairy-Freez and that, just like the Dairy-Freez in Ohio, it would be sure to have Fudge Dips. "Hey," I said, suddenly struck. "When did you go out for ice cream anyhow?"

"Oh," Nell said, "the night you were in the hospital. A friend of Kit's took us. Dan Flannery. He works at the printing plant, too."

"Is he her boyfriend?"

"He's her friend, Mia. They work together. Not everything in life is like an Archie and Veronica comic book."

The heat made my shirt stick to the swing. I leaned forward to stretch, peering out through the branches of the catalpa tree. Out there everything was waiting for me. The old sidewalks, buckled with maple roots, the Dairy-Freez, the dime store, the wide, pearly sky. I picked up my report card. "I'm promoted," I said glumly. "I'm supposed to get Mrs. Weill for homeroom. A Kraut."

Nell slammed her book shut. She reached up under her glasses and rubbed her eyelids with two fingers. "Mia," she said, "it almost physically pains me to hear you say such ignorant things. It's exactly why it would be good for you to have a teacher from Germany. To broaden your world view."

"She's from Switzerland."

"Oh," Nell said. "Still. Anything would help."

Just talking about school was making me itch again. I rubbed my hands across my knees, scratching them on the tough calluses I had built up from shinnying over the scales of the palm trees. It felt like touching animal hide.

"Anyway"—Nell continued—"that's an excellent school you attend. You've been privileged, Mia, and if I were you, I'd be crossing my fingers that everything works out for you to go back there."

I stared at my knees, remembering the eggplant smell and the way the door to our classroom closed with a small, final click. "Yeah, well, if it's so great," I said, "how come you and Bibi go to the French school instead?"

"To take advantage of another cultural opportunity. To reach out to life." She sounded airy, like my mom. "And let me just tell you something. If you find school as you have known it to be oppressive, just try going to school in a podunk place like this. Did you know it's still against the law to even teach evolution in schools in this state?"

I shrugged. I had no idea what she was talking about, but I was tired of her attacking Ionia. A soap opera theme drifted out from a neighbor's television. Heat waves dazzled from the roofs of parked cars. Deep in the privet hedge a few locusts began to sing. Ionia was what it was. "You're just anti-American," I said to Nell. "You can't ever say that anything American is good."

"Mia, that's not the point. You're the daughter of a scientist. You, of all people, should be smart enough to know there's something the matter with an educational system that gives you no alternative to Adam and Eve in this day and age."

"What's wrong with Adam and Eve?" I couldn't figure out how they'd gotten into this argument at all. In my Children's Bible, I had read the story of the Garden of Eden over and over. My favorite part was about how a mist rose up from the ground to water the earth because God had not thought to invent rain yet. I liked the idea that He had to tinker around with things to get them working right, just like anybody's dad trying to build a bookshelf or assemble a bicycle.

"Nothing's *wrong* with Adam and Eve." Nell patted at her hair clips again. "It's a fine story, rich in mythology. But I simply don't choose to believe it really happened, and I'm glad I have other information available to me."

"You don't believe in Adam and Eve?"

"Not literally, no."

"Do you believe in God?"

Nell laughed. "What is this, an inquisition?"

"Well, do you?"

She sighed. "No," she said, "at least not in the conventional sense. I believe in a mysterious, creative force, a spirit within. But somebody who talks to you from the sky? Who can scrape up some dust and make a human being? No."

"So," I said, surprised by the iciness of my own voice, "then you're a Communist, I suppose."

Nell held both hands in the air. She had removed two hair clips over her forehead, and a ringlet dangled between her eyes. "Right, Senator McCarthy," she said, "you caught me red-handed."

Senator McCarthy? I stared at her.

"Well, maybe not red-handed," she said. "I'm not a member of the Communist party, but I do admire certain aspects of communism as a philosophy. Maybe that's just pink-handed." She laughed. The curl bobbled over her nose.

So, it was all a joke to her, the Dairy-Freez, Adam and Eve, anything I thought was good. I looked up at President Kennedy, but he was gone, his outline switched back to a stagecoach. No matter how fast I blinked I could not make his nose and chin appear from the spoked wheels. I felt my own chin tremble. "I wish Mom were here," I said into the still air. "I wish she could hear the things you're saying."

"She'd agree with most of it," Nell said. "As you would know if you ever paid attention at the dinner table. Tune in sometime, Mia. You could learn a lot."

I thought of our dinners in Beirut and how the words flew around—"theory!" "thrust fault!" "theological!"— making a glaze slide over my brain. I could feel it happen as I sat there, running my fork over my plate of kousa squash. I guessed it was much like being hypnotized, a restful, removed feeling.

Sooner or later, though, my mom would stop the conversation and say, "Mia! Tell us about your day." It always took me a minute. I was like a diver, down deep, who has to drift to the surface.

"Uh, Connie Blakey got bitten by a centipede on the playground," I could finally manage to say, "and her throat closed up so she had to be rushed to the infirmary for a shot." That would launch them on a new set of topics—"arthropods!" "allergens!" "antihistamines!"—and I was released to sink back into my trance.

Sometimes I watched them, from my end of the table, the way they laughed and argued, leaning forward to speak so that their faces were caught for a minute, softened and rosy, in the candlelight, and I thought it might make my heart break. I loved them. I just wanted them to be normal.

Nell picked up her book and gathered stray hair clips. "Comb-out time," she said, standing up. There was the sound of crunching gravel in the driveway behind us.

"Now what?" Nell said. She leaned down across the swing to peek through the catalpa branches. With her hair still pinned up, the back of her neck looked pale and exposed. The deep hollow just beneath her hairline was beautiful. It would break my heart to think of her as a Communist.

"God," Nell said, "it's Kit, with Mr. Flannery! I thought

she wasn't getting out of the hospital until tomorrow." She turned and headed for the screen door. "I'd better tell Bibi. God! I've got to go get these things out of my hair."

I turned around and knelt backward on the swing. Through the branches I could see a light blue car, stopped almost next to the tree. Inside sat Kit, her thin face turned sideways, looking at Mr. Flannery. He was talking and smiling, and his hands beat once on the steering wheel as if he were telling a story. I liked his looks, his broad face and toothy grin. They didn't seem in any hurry to get out of the car. Kit shook her head sadly at something he said. She sat awkwardly, half turned, in her seat and slanted forward at the same time. I wondered if her arms hurt and if they were both in slings. How would she eat her food or brush her hair? How would she put her nightgown on?

The locusts began to sing again. Kit smiled faintly. Mr. Flannery put his hand under her chin and kissed her. A long kiss. I touched my mouth. I was hot all over. The noon whistle blasted at the cement works and startled birds right out of the trees, but the kiss went on. Overhead, through the branches, I could see the moon, almost gone now. It was like a watermark on paper.

I smiled. If Nell had been wrong about Kit having a boyfriend, then she could be wrong about everything.

CHAPTER
4

I had a dream that my parents were riding in a big black car, an old-fashioned car, shaped like a bowler hat. My mom was driving, and my dad was sitting next to her, smoking his pipe. For some reason they both were wearing leis. I stood on the sidewalk, and they drove right past me. When they got to the end of the street, there was a cliff and my mom drove straight over the edge. But instead of falling, the car flew. "Come back," I yelled, but the car flew on. My mom stuck her arm out the window to wave, and it was a skeleton's arm. I could see fingerbones and a white knob of elbow against the gray sky.

I woke up, crying and snarled in the sheet. It was light outside. I thought I smelled my dad's sweet, grainy pipe tobacco in the air, but after a second I recognized it as the scent of spray starch. My sisters were ironing clothes in the kitchen, just outside my bedroom door. I could hear them whispering, and I could hear the hiss and thump of the steam iron. I wiped my eyes with the edge of the pillowcase. Today was Saturday, and Bibi and Nell were going away to Boston. It was the day I'd once dreaded, but now I felt a thrill, like a small electrical jolt, inside my chest: I was going to have Mr. Flannery and Kit all to myself.

Ever since I'd seen them kiss, I wanted to be around them. I was trying to understand about the moment when things changed, when people's lips went from shaping everyday words like *orange juice* or *raincoat* to crushing together as if they had no choice. It was mysterious, and it made my pulse beat like a drum in my ears. Suddenly my aunt was prettier, her freckles translucent, like pastry crumbs, against her pale skin. My sisters polished her nails, and I noticed how delicate her fingers looked, curling from the gauze mitts at the ends of her plaster casts. She could have been a heroine in an old-time movie, and when I helped her by zipping up her sundress each morning, it changed everything to think of her bony, speckled back as a back that somebody loved.

The steam iron made a sound like a drawn-out sigh. I climbed out of bed, and the floorboards were already warm under my feet. In the kitchen Nell was folding up the ironing board, and Bibi was frying bacon at the stove. She had a dish towel on her head so the smoke wouldn't get into her hair.

"Ask me nicely, and I'll give you the crisps," she told me.

"Please, may I have the crisps?" I said.

"Say 'pretty please.'"

I knew that she was teasing me just to give me some attention, to make it up to me for going off to Boston, and I felt a pang of guilt about not being sadder. The kitchen was hazy with dim sunlight and bacon grease. Nell and Bibi, in their long bathrobes, seemed to float through the room. They made me think of the nuns in the hospital when I had my tonsils out. Bibi smiled at me. I felt bad that I didn't even care about the crisps that she was scraping out of the pan.

"Pretty please," I said.

At breakfast Kit told us that we should call Mr. Flannery Dan. She pronounced it in two syllables—"Dayin"—and I heard his name thrum in the air after she said it. I looked at my sisters. They nodded at Kit and went on eating, not seeming to hear anything out of the ordinary. This just confirmed what I'd already thought: that I was joined into Kit's romance in some special, meaningful way, that it was partly mine to share. I knew for certain that whenever Mr. Flannery rested his hand on my aunt's shoulder, I felt the warmth from his palm sink down through the layers of my own skin. When he smiled, it was like something private, passing between us.

"Mia," Nell said, "you're blushing."

"No, I'm not." I knew that I was. My cheeks were tingling. I picked up my juice glass and pretended to study the Rocky and Bullwinkle figures printed on the side.

"You are flushed," Kit said. "I hope you're not feverish."

I shook my head, still peering intently into my juice glass.

"All right," Kit said, "but you be sure and tell me if you're not feeling well." She scooted her chair back from the table and stood up. The cast on her right arm covered her elbow, but the one on her left was shorter, allowing her to bend her arm. She was able to eat and to brush her teeth, but she could not write her name or hold a newspaper or apply her own lipstick. It would be awhile before she could go back to coloring maps, and I wondered if Dan Flannery stared, bereft, at her empty desk while he was working. His sweetheart. His darling! My face burned hotter.

"Mia, really, I am worried," Kit said. "You're almost glassy-eyed."

"I'm okay." I licked a finger and used it to stab at toast crumbs on my plate.

"Well," Kit said, "I hope so. Maybe we should take your temperature anyhow."

"I wouldn't worry about it, Kit," Bibi said. "This happens to her all the time. It's a phase."

"Yeah," Nell said. "It's the effect of *l'esprit mal tourné*!"

Kit looked confused. I ground toast crumbs with my teeth.

"A dirty mind." Nell translated for Kit. "It shows up on her face. We used to laugh about it all the time in Beirut. Anything can set her off. Fried eggs. Toilet brushes."

"Meatballs!" Bibi said. "Fountain pens! Just look at her blush."

They all turned toward me. I put my hands over my flaming cheeks. "I'm glad you're leaving," I said, pushing my chair back and standing up. "I'm not going to miss you. I don't even care!"

In my room I poked through my clothes, looking for something nice to wear to the airport. At last I was going somewhere. I pulled crumpled skirts and blouses out of my green canvas suitcase and tried to smooth them out. Since I'd been at Kit's, I'd only unpacked some shorts and nightgowns, the things I'd need until my parents came to get me. Now I looked at the wrinkled clothes in confusion. When you opened the suitcase, you could smell the damp, sweet air of our apartment in Beirut. If I wore these clothes now, it was almost the same as saying that my mom and dad would never come. I held up my favorite skirt, pale blue, printed with darker blue forget-me-nots. Right now it was creased with diagonal lines that made it hang crookedly, but even so, it was pretty, like a bouquet of forget-me-nots tossed against the sky. I folded the skirt up carefully and put it back into the suitcase, along with the other things I'd pulled out. When I'd zipped it shut and clicked the little tab lock into place, I leaned over and kissed it to seal the vow: I wouldn't open it again until my parents came.

My yellow checked Bermuda shorts were from a summer ago, and they felt tight, hiking up against my bottom, but I chose to wear them anyway because they had a yellow shirt with a matching checked collar to go with them. I brushed my hair hard and smiled at myself in the mirror. My hair had a few reddish glints that stood out from its paper bag color, and my eyes, staring right back at me, looked deep and secretive, like a cat's. Maybe I was getting prettier, too, along with Kit. Love! The drumbeat started again. Bibi and Nell were just wrong. Dirty thoughts had no place in the romance I shared with Kit and Dan Flannery. We didn't need the images that Jill Pillsworth had tried to plant in my mind, those embarrassing bobbling and stiffening body parts. We had everything we wanted: lingering shoulder rubs and long lip-crusher kisses. The drums quickened. I could hardly wait for the ride home from the airport, the three of us, alone together, at last.

A car horn tooted out front. I smiled mysteriously into the mirror, tugged at my shorts, and skipped out, ready.

Outside, rounding the side of the catalpa tree, I stopped still in my tracks. Dan Flannery wasn't alone. He stood next to his car with a scrawny-looking girl younger than I was. "Mia! Here's somebody I want you to meet."

I walked slowly toward them, conscious suddenly of how I must have looked, skipping that way, my bangs flapping against my forehead. I felt like a big canary in my yellow clothes. The girl had on a white sundress with red, blue, and yellow polka dots that I envied instantly. It was like the wrapper on Wonder bread.

"Patsy," Dan Flannery said, "this is Mia. Mia, Patsy." He smiled at both of us. His teeth were white and even, like tiles. "My daughter," he added.

I stood still. The locusts trilled sharply in the bushes, and the sun beat down on the catalpa leaves, causing them to droop. Patsy held out her hand, and I shook it. It felt weightless, like holding a biscuit. She had that straight blond hair that seems almost white and translucent pale skin. She stared back at me, and her eyes were the same flat blue as his. Dan Flannery had a daughter.

"Excuse me," I said. "I have to go help with the suitcases."

"Oh, I can do that," Dan Flannery said, but I was already gone, speeding back into the house. My sisters' bags were lined up in the hallway, and I sidestepped them to get to Kit's room. She was just coming out of her door, with her green dress sliding down on her shoulders.

"Just who I needed," she said. "My zipper-upper." She turned around, and I zipped the dress, lifting the ends of her hair out of the way.

"Where did this Patsy come from?" I said.

Kit turned around to look at me. "She's Dan's daughter."

"I know, but where did she *come* from?"

"Well," Kit said, "she lives over in Una. With her mama."

"Her mama? He's *married*?" My voice rose.

"He was," Kit said.

The screen door slammed. "Let's get this show on the road," Dan Flannery called. "You-all have a plane to catch."

Kit touched my arm. "I'll explain it later," she said. "We'll talk about this later."

On the ride to the airport I sulked, sitting in the center of the backseat, my feet balanced on the hump in the floor. I could list all the people I hated just then. My sisters on either side of me, about to fly away. Dan Flannery, smiling that way at my aunt and me when he already had a wife and daughter. And worst of all, Patsy herself, riding in the front seat, talking baby talk the whole way. "Oh, Daddy," she said in her little piping voice, "you silly billy!"

"I think I might be carsick," I said. "I think I have to throw up."

Dan Flannery steered over to the edge of the highway, and I scrambled out into the thick, hot air that smelled like cows. I bent over, but nothing happened; just a bitterness came in my mouth. When I stood up, I saw the cows, pressing close to the barbwire fence to look at me with their big, patient faces.

"I hate them all," I told the cows. "I wish I could stay here with you."

Nell called my name, and I had to go, but they didn't make me sit in the middle anymore. Now I had a window.

I had been to the Nashville airport once before, the night Bibi and Nell and I flew in. Then, it seemed mysterious, the tower beacon sweeping across the dark sky, the trip across the tarmac in the hot, damp air to meet our unknown aunt. But today, in daylight, it was just an airport. My sisters were leaving, and I wanted to find something to mark it, to make it memorable, but really there was nothing. It was like every airport I'd ever seen: a few big hangars, a crisscross of asphalt strips, and a film of airplane exhaust, visible in the sky.

At the gate Bibi clutched me to her and then passed me over to Nell. "Everything's going to be okay," Nell whispered.

"Yeah," I said.

"We'll call you soon," Bibi said. "And we'll write."

"And you can write to us, too," Nell said. "You have the address."

"Yeah," I said again.

We stood, just sliding our feet on the shiny tile floor. The door opened, and there was a rush of wind, all those propellers turning.

"I want to go with you," I whispered, but no sound came out. You couldn't hear anything above the engine noise. They hugged me again, and then they were caught up in the line of other passengers. I watched them walk toward the plane, their gold hair whipping around in the hot wind. The door closed, and there I stood, left with three people I hardly knew.

"Daddy," Patsy said, "my tummy is so, so hungry. Can we get my ice-cream soda now?"

In the airport coffee shop I ate every bite of my cheeseburger and rooted with my straw for the last drops of chocolate milk shake. Patsy was sitting on my right, and for someone who was hungry, she ate at an excruciating pace. She dipped the long-handled spoon into her vanilla soda, lifted a tiny white blob, and then sucked, daintily, on the spoon's tip. On the plate in front of her was a chicken club sandwich, cut into four wedges and anchored with cellophane-topped toothpicks. One-quarter of the sandwich had two small bites taken from it, but the rest was untouched, and I eyed it covetously. I felt as if I could eat and eat here, with the smells of potato chips and coffee, the clatter of dishes and American voices.

"That was the first milk shake I've had in three years," I told Patsy. She looked at me briefly and went on spooning.

"How old are you anyhow?" I asked.

"Ten." She pronounced it "tin."

"What grade are you going to be in?"

"Fifth, at St. Brigid's."

"Oh," I said. "A Catholic school?"

Her eyes flicked over at me. "Yes," she said.

"President Kennedy is Catholic," I said.

"Duh," she said. "Everybody knows that." She turned back to her soda.

I hated her more than ever, but I wanted to win. I wanted to get her attention. "That's a nice bracelet you have," I said.

It worked. She turned toward me, holding out her pale, sticklike arm, twisting the bracelet on her wrist. "Guess what it's made out of," she said.

"I don't know."

"Go on, guess."

"Silver?"

"Ha-ha, it's the rim off a peach can," she said. "I made it myself."

"Really."

"It always fools people that don't know any better."

I sat back in my chair, unwrapping a sugar cube to suck on. The waitress came by with our check. She had to wear a paper cap and an apron shaped like an aspen leaf. She winked when she saw me looking. Probably she thought we were a mom and a dad and two daughters, just something regular. Kit got up to use the ladies' room, and Dan Flannery went over to the counter to pay.

"Do you want that?" I asked Patsy, pointing to the uneaten sandwich triangles in front of her.

"Yes," she said.

"But we're leaving in a minute."

"My daddy will get them to put it in a doggie bag for me," she said. "He always does." She went on eating her soda methodically, pursing her mouth over the spoon. I couldn't stand it any longer.

"So your parents are divorced," I said. "Poor you."

She licked ice cream off her top lip. "No, they're not."

"Duh," I said. "They are, too."

"They're never getting a divorce. My mama said so."

"How come he's with my aunt then? How come he has a *girlfriend*?"

Patsy shrugged. "He always does. He always has girl-friends when he and my mama aren't getting along." She put her spoon down and looked up at me with her flat, satisfied eyes. "But see, he always comes back. To us."

On the ride home I just wanted to warn Kit. You couldn't ever trust him. Now I could see it so easily. His cold eyes. His false, slippery smile. I sat by myself in the backseat, alert. Each time he snaked his hand along the edge of the seat to squeeze my aunt's shoulder, I drummed my sneakers on the floor of the car, a warning.

"Mia, please stop that noise," he said.

I saw his cold eyes in the mirror. I drummed my feet again. "It's a free country," I told him.

"Mia!" Kit said. "Stop that right now!"

"Yeah," Patsy said. "It's Daddy's car. He's the boss of it."

"She's just upset," Kit said in a low voice to Dan. "You know, she's upset about her sisters leaving."

I added her to my list. I hated everyone. I didn't care. I sat alone in the backseat, glaring out the window. Just speeding past the cows in the field, I wanted to cry. They were still bunched together, waiting by the same fence, as if they hoped I was coming back.

CHAPTER

5

We had a heat wave that made the sky darken every afternoon. Thunder crackled, distantly, behind the low rust-colored hills outside town, but it never rained.

"I'd like to crawl right out of my skin," Kit said. She had to pace around the room because the humid air made her casts itch. I tried poking a broom straw under the plaster to scratch her arms, but it didn't do any good. When she got tired of pacing, she took a Nehi from the refrigerator and flopped down onto a kitchen chair, pressing the cold bottle against the side of her neck. I sat across from her, watching beads of water slide off the bottle and down her collarbone. I felt bad. If it weren't for me, she wouldn't have two broken arms and she wouldn't be sitting here, looking like a loony person.

"I wish I could do something," I said, "help you some-how."

She had been staring into the electric fan on the kitchen table, but now she looked at me with her worried gray eyes, and I felt a rush of fear that she was going to tell the truth: There was plenty I could do to help. For one, I could speak to Dan Flannery instead of shutting myself in my room night after night, trying to wish away the fact that he was here, with her, listening to Henry Mancini records in the living room.

"He's married!" I'd shouted at Kit when we came home from the trip to the airport.

"Well, technically, yes, but—"

"Married!"

"Now it sounds bad when you put it that way, but really, it's not a marriage. It's over. But she's a practicing Catholic, and it's not simple. It's very involved. It's—"

"You could find somebody else," I told her. "Somebody better."

But every night there he was again. He brought us hamburgers from the Rebel-Maid, and we ate them at the kitchen table. I didn't talk. He thought it earned him something, bringing us those hamburgers, little pads of meat. When I finished chewing, I said, "Thank you," looking at nobody. Then I went to my room.

At night the pine boards on the walls of my room seemed to soak up the lamplight, casting everything in a strange, lemony shadow. The music that came out of the transistor radio sounded thin and far away. If I held it up to my ear, the small voices, sputtering with static, made me feel the same as when an airplane flew overhead, at night, all lit up, and I'd understand it was full of people going someplace who didn't know about me, on the earth below them.

My parents had been gone four weeks, my sisters had been gone sixteen days. I still could not wear the dresses and skirts locked up in my suitcase. And every day, without warning, there were new things I couldn't do. I couldn't eat Wint-O-Green Life Savers now or read *Dondi* in the morning funnies or use Kit's rosewater and glycerin lotion to soften the calluses on my knees. Nobody gave me these orders, but I didn't just choose them either. I'd be peeling back the foil on the Life Savers, ready to pry the next one out of the pack, and I would just know it: Stop now if you want your mom and dad back.

Across the kitchen table I watched Kit chew on her lip, trying to think of how to answer me. I couldn't stand to talk about Dan Flannery again. I couldn't tell her anything about the orders I had to obey. Her damp bangs ruffled a little each time the fan pivoted in her direction. Finally she held up her unopened Nehi bottle. "Do me a favor," she said, "put this one back in the icebox and get me a nice, cool one instead."

I jumped up from my chair and took the bottle. My heart felt light. This was something I could do.

Mrs. Swope drove me to Kroger's to get groceries. Her car was enormous and had deep, comfortable seats. I could hardly see over the dashboard, and neither could

Mrs. Swope, who leaned forward, squinting and gripping the steering wheel with both hands, as if it were holding her in place. Even in the heat she wore a long-sleeved print dress with her mustard seed pin on the collar.

"I don't like the looks of that sky," she said.

The clouds were closing in just the way they did every afternoon, but the tinted blue glass across the top of the car's windshield exaggerated the effect, making the sky seem dark and bruised. If you looked out the side windows, though, things were just ordinary, a dull, steamy gray. I didn't know whether to point this out or not. I was trying to be extra polite today to make up for the way Mrs. Swope had last seen me, pitching a fit.

"Folks call this a tornado sky," she added.

"In Beirut, where I used to live, the sea would turn three different colors before a storm," I said, surprising myself. My voice sounded so sad. I thought of the wind shaking the slanted palm trees, making the fronds clack together like percussion music. "Green," I said, "then turquoise, then silver."

"I don't guess I'll ever get to see that," Mrs. Swope said.

Kroger's smelled just how I remembered from Ohio, a good mix of fruit and floor wax and coffee. Over the bread aisle a giant picture of the Sunbeam girl smiled down at us, and she was like an old friend. I pulled out the list that Kit had dictated to me. Some things she had specified by brands—Purity Dairies milk, Frosty Morn bacon, Dutch cleanser—but other things I could choose myself as long as I didn't spend more than twenty dollars. The trick, Kit had told me, was to figure that each item I bought would cost an average of fifty cents. That meant that all I had to do was count everything I put in my basket and divide the total in half to estimate how much I'd spent. Right away I picked out raisin bread and powdered sugar doughnuts and a packaged angel food cake, things I hadn't seen for three years.

"This is so great!" I said to Mrs. Swope. We walked along slowly, pushing our carts up and down the aisles. Mrs. Swope spent a long time finding just what she wanted: tiny cans of black-eyed peas, loin pork chops with no gristle, a package of saltines with unsalted tops. She had to take off her glasses to read the prices, and it made her face look different, flattened and tender.

I carefully counted everything that I tossed into my cart, but after a while it got confusing. Dial soap came in single bars or in packets with three bars stuck together. I couldn't figure out if it counted as one item or three. Also, chicken pot pies were three for sixty-nine cents, but we only needed two. It was turning out that shopping was too much like an arithmetic problem. I looked at the things in the cart, and they didn't seem so exciting anymore. You just paid money for them and then you used them up and you had to do it all over again. It seemed like too much trouble, even for angel food cake or Bosco.

At the back of the store the air was icy from the big, open freezers. Mrs. Swope was looking at packages of vegetables. I scraped frost off the side of the freezer with my fingernail. My arms were covered with goose bumps. I just wanted to pay for things and go. Mrs. Swope picked up a package of lima beans and peered at it. She took off her glasses and held the package out at arm's length, squinting.

"What?" I said.

"Oh, honey, I take too long," Mrs. Swope said. "I just don't see where it says 'Fordhook.' I only buy Fordhook."

"Right *here*." I took the package of lima beans from her and held it close to her face, pointing to the word. *"Ford. Hook."*

"Thank you." Mrs. Swope took the package back from me and leaned down to place it, carefully, among the few other things in her cart. I could see the curved ridge of her backbone through her print dress. Her hair was a faded color, like dove feathers. I was ashamed of myself for being so impatient, but it was too late now. Nothing ever worked out how I wanted it to. My skin felt chilled and heavy, suddenly. I hoped I wasn't going to cry, but tears were already pooling in my eyes. They trailed down, warm against my cold cheeks, and I dabbed them away with the back of my hand. Mrs. Swope had moved on ahead of me, pushing her cart toward the cash register. I saw my face reflected in the tilted strip of mirror above the freezers. I thought of what my mom used to say: "Your face is a mask of woe!"

"Mom," I whispered, and I cried harder, just watching my mouth shape the word.

As we rode home, heat lightning was starting to flicker across the sky. The ovenlike air in the car felt good, thawing my skin. Mrs. Swope gripped the wheel and drove in silence. If she noticed that my face was streaked from crying, she didn't say so. Just a few blocks from Kit's house, rain began to splatter against the windshield. Mrs. Swope slowed the car down and turned on the wipers. We inched down the road until the rain got harder, and suddenly hail, the size of mothballs, was falling, bouncing crazily off the car. Mrs. Swope pulled over to the side of the road, and we sat there listening to the rattle of hailstones. She kept her hands wrapped tightly around the steering wheel. The joints in her fingers looked stiff and shiny, as if they might be coated with wax paper.

After a couple of minutes the hail stopped, but Mrs. Swope didn't start up the car. I watched lightning flash in blue streaks through the tinted windshield. Mrs. Swope leaned down and fumbled through a grocery bag that was next to my feet. She pulled out a package of cookies, Social Teas.

"I think we need us a little treat," she said. "We deserve it."

It took her awhile to work the cardboard package open. She held it out to me, and just looking at the row of scallop-edged cookies made my stomach rumble, I was so hungry. But as I was about to reach for one, the order came out of the air: Stop, don't take one.

"Maybe you don't like these plain old things." Mrs. Swope's hand shook slightly as she went on holding the package out for me. "They're all I buy anymore. Plain old cookies for a plain old lady!"

"You're not old," I said. I plucked a cookie from the pack and clasped it in my lap. I felt dizzy. My hands were sweating. Everything would be okay, I decided, if I didn't *eat* the cookie.

"Oh, honey," Mrs. Swope said, "I'm old as the hills, but I don't care."

She started the motor and eased the car back onto the road. I smelled the hot, wet pavement and the strong peaty scent of soaked ground. We passed by yards littered with soggy rose petals. I wanted a friend who would play outdoors with me, scooping up rose petals and floating them in the flooded ditches. But I didn't know anybody except Patsy Flannery, and I could not imagine her crawling around in the wet grass or taking off her sandals to splash her bony white toes in the mud. Anyway I hoped never to see her smug, pasty face again. I thought about Jill Pillsworth, and I felt a pang. Even though she teased me and told me lies, she knew how to have fun. She was the one who'd had the idea of turning cartwheels across the Corniche in the late afternoons, just after the prayer call came from the mosque and all the Moslems had to bow toward Mecca. They dropped down on the sidewalks, praying and trailing their burnoose sleeves in the dust, while Jill and I flipped over and over all around them, letting our skirts fly up, showing off our flower-sprigged Spanky pants, feeling thrilled.

I sank back into the deep seat of Mrs. Swope's car. I was too tired to think anymore. Today had already been too confusing, too up and down, too happy and sad. The best thing would be to go on riding in this warm, plushy car for the rest of the day, listening to the motor tick, gazing at a sky that was permanently blue.

"Here we are," said Mrs. Swope.

We turned into Kit's driveway and stopped suddenly. There was an unfamiliar car parked in front of us, a dark green sedan with a white license plate that said "U.S. Government" across the bottom.

"Whoa, who could that be?" I asked.

Mrs. Swope didn't answer. She took off her glasses and massaged her eyes with two wax paper fingers. Kit came around the side of the catalpa tree, followed by two men, one in an army uniform, one in a gray suit. And then I knew. I watched the three of them walking solemn-faced toward me, and my stomach cramped up with dread. I wanted to jump out of the car and run away from whatever they had to say, but I sat there, frozen, listening to the crunch of the gravel under their feet.

The car door on my side opened, and Kit stuck her head in. "Mia," she said, "this is Mr. Burton. He came from Washington to talk to you about your mom and dad."

I knew that anything I was about to hear was my own fault. I was still holding the Social Tea, crumbled and damp, in my sweating hand. The instructions had been clear: Don't take the cookie. Don't *take* the cookie.

"Mia?"

Mrs. Swope had left the windshield wipers going although the rain had stopped, and I stared at their back-and-forth motion. This was what I would always remember about this moment, I decided, the singsong scraping of the wipers and the way they dipped together in perfect time, like dancing partners who weren't aware that there was anybody else in the world.

"Mia." The man in the gray suit leaned in through the door of the car to speak to me. "I'm afraid I don't have any news to tell you about your parents, dear. I just need to ask you a few things."

I looked up. Everyone was looking back at me, waiting for me to say something. The man in the uniform was holding his hat in his hand. He winked at me.

"I have to go to the bathroom," I said.

At the sink I washed every trace of cookie off my hand, letting the water run hotter and hotter until my skin had a pink, boiled look. I had learned my lesson. I would never cheat again, never try to change the rules, no matter what they were or when they came. I would wear my old shorts until they were in tatters. I would do what I had to do.

There was a tap at the door, and Kit came in.

"I just wanted to tell you how sorry I am that you had a scare like that," she said. "I didn't think."

"It's okay." I picked up the edge of a towel and began to dry my hands.

"I worry about you, Mia. You seem so hard on yourself. You're just a little girl, sweetie. No matter what happens, you can't carry the weight of the world on your shoulders."

I bent down, studying my fingers as I rubbed them with the towel.

"Okay," Kit said. "Well." She turned to go out of the room. I hesitated, but when no orders came out of the air to stop me, I bounded forward and flung my arms around her ribs, burying my face in the clean, chalky smell of her cotton sundress. My joints tingled, as if I'd been running hard or riding my bike up a hill. I never asked for the weight of the world; it just seemed to be mine. I opened my eyes and watched the small clouds of steam float against the bathroom ceiling and disappear.

"I know," Kit whispered. "I know."

CHAPTER

6

Mr. Burton was waiting for me out on the porch. The sun had come out, making water drops shine in the trees.

"Here, we dried off a chair for you, dear," he said. He sounded so kind it made me shy. He had come from Washington to see me. I stared at his polished shoes, now coated with wet grass clippings.

"So, Mia," he said, "have you ever seen anybody take shorthand before?"

I nodded, still looking down. "Bibi," I said. "She learned it from a book. In three languages."

Mr. Burton whistled. "Very impressive," he said.

"She's my sister."

"Oh, I know. I've spoken to her on the phone several times. And I'll be flying up to Boston in the next couple of days to talk to both of your sisters."

I looked up then.

He smiled. "We're going to solve this, Mia. We're doing everything we can."

Everything about him was strong: his wide shoulders in his blue pin-striped suit; his sturdy tanned face; even his smile, a straight slash across his jaw. He was going to solve this.

"Anyway," Mr. Burton said, "I'm afraid I don't take shorthand myself—"

"Of course not!" I said indignantly. It was unthinkable, his large, square hands forming little chicken scratches in a notebook.

"But fortunately Corporal Pawley, who drove me out here from the airport, happens to be a shorthand expert, and he's going to help me out by writing down our conversation. So if you don't mind, we'll just wait a minute for him. He's unloading groceries for your aunt."

I wondered if Mr. Burton knew the whole story of Kit's broken arms. The water tower was visible from where we were sitting. It flashed in the sunlight on the hillside, high above the scrubby pine trees. Mr. Burton glanced down at a pile of papers he was holding in his lap. His face was bronzed, except for the fine white squint lines at the corners of his eyes. I had the feeling that he knew everything: my grades in school; how I showed my underpants to praying Moslems; even the way my blood quickened when I thought about body parts. I looked down again, blushing and thrilled. I tightened my leg muscles until they cramped. I wanted to run off the porch for a minute, out into the hot, wet yard to stretch, but the screen door opened and Corporal Pawley came out.

"Hey," he said. He walked over to the porch swing and sat down, facing us. He took out a small spiral notebook and a yellow pencil. "Stenographer, reporting for duty," he said.

"Okay then." Mr. Burton turned toward me. He touched my shoulder and looked at me with a solemn, steady expression. "Mia, anything you can remember may help us find out what's happened to your parents. So say whatever comes to mind. Anything. Everything. Got it?"

I nodded. I tapped my heels against the cement floor. My legs felt tight as wires, ready to snap.

"Let's start by just talking about the morning your mother and father left for Greece. Did they take a taxi to the airport?"

"No, Mr. Clarke took them in his car."

"Who is Mr. Clarke?"

"He teaches with my dad. Geology." Corporal Pawley's head was bent down as he scribbled in his notebook. He had curly hair, but it was cut so short it stuck up in swirls and ripples. It made me think of a coral reef.

"So they left in Mr. Clarke's car." Mr. Burton continued. "And how did they seem? Excited? Nervous? Anything unusual?"

I thought for a minute. "They were just sleepy. It was so early in the morning they could hardly wake up. Alize made them coffee, but she always makes it like Turkish coffee, and it tastes like dirt. They had to spit it out down the drain when she wasn't looking."

"And Alize is?"

"The woman who comes to stay with us every time my mom and dad go away. She's Armenian." It surprised me to realize that I'd almost forgotten Alize. She used to fix me snacks of tangerine slices, sprinkled with sugar, and she laughed whenever I showed off, doing my pretend tap dancing. "Shirley Temple!" she said. "I know!" Her teeth were big and stained from strong coffee. And her gums showed when she laughed. I thought she looked like a horse, in a nice way.

When my mom and dad didn't come back on the day they were supposed to, Alize got scared because her husband wanted the money my parents were going to pay her. Her husband came to the apartment door and banged on it. He shouted in Armenian. We sat, quietly, in the living room. Alize hid her face in her hands. Bibi and I were on the sofa, and she had her arm around me. Across the Corniche I could see the waves rolling in. I thought my mom and dad were just late. I thought they'd come on the plane that night or first thing in the morning. Alize's husband began to ring the doorbell over and over. Nell jumped up to telephone down to the concierge for help. I felt hypnotized by the doorbell. It chimed, again and again, two tones that sounded like the beginning of "Swing Low, Sweet Chariot."

"Okay," Mr. Burton said. "Now we're going to back-track a little." He peered down at his notes. "How did your mother and father get the idea for this trip, do you recall?"

"My mom wanted to. She drew on these charts, planning it all the time because she was studying navigation."

"Where was she studying?"

"I don't know. At the university, I think. Bibi and Nell might know. They probably know."

Mr. Burton shrugged his huge shoulders and frowned down at his papers. Corporal Pawley had stopped writing. He stretched his arms and winked at me. I wasn't helping them at all. They had come this whole way to talk to me, and I didn't have anything to tell them. I tried to think.

"Maybe, if you could find a copy of my mom's charts, you could retrace their route." My heart began to pump. I was on to something. "She did so many charts. I bet there are still some in our apartment in Beirut. You could fly there and get one!"

Mr. Burton smiled and shook his head. "That's very good thinking, Mia, but we already have a copy of their intended route. They had to file one with the charter company when they took the sailboat." He rubbed his forehead with his knuckles. "What we can't figure out is why they didn't follow their plans. There were no big storms, no accidents reported. What could have made them change their course?"

With my mom, I thought, it could have been almost anything that made her shift course—a school of dolphins swimming by, an island on the horizon, whatever path the moonlight made across the water—but I didn't know how to say this the right way to Mr. Burton. I watched him rub his eyelids with his square fingertips. He would save my mom and dad if I could give him the right clues, the key words.

"It's something about what my mom believes in," I said cautiously. I was afraid of making her sound silly. I tried to remember the word she spelled for me the day we talked about churches, the important-sounding word for someone who follows beauty. It began with *a*, but now the rest of it kept slipping just out of reach of my memory.

Mr. Burton stopped rubbing his eyes and looked at me. "Your mom?" he said. "You mean you think your mom might have changed her plans due to her beliefs?"

I nodded. He was interested now. He leaned forward in his chair. His skin smelled like limes.

"What beliefs do you mean?" he asked.

Corporal Pawley sat with his pencil poised, waiting to write. I still couldn't think of the word.

"Anything you can tell us will help," Mr. Burton said. "Anything that comes to mind."

I tightened my leg muscles again. This seemed so important. I thought of how to say it. "It's the way you should live your life. It should be something special. You shouldn't be afraid to follow the path of the light."

"The path of the light," Mr. Burton repeated. "Mia, does this have something to do with religion?"

"No," I said. "It's different." I hoped he wasn't going to ask me which church we went to.

"Well, tell me, did you ever hear your parents talk about politics?"

I thought of those dinner table discussions where the words buzzed through the air, over my head. "Yes," I said. "All the time."

"So," he said, "could the path of the light have something to do with politics, do you think?"

"I don't know." I was confused now. I wished I had paid attention at the table. "I thought it was from the moon."

"The moon?" Mr. Burton said. "The moon." He looked thoughtful. "You know, Mia, it occurs to me that several different countries have the moon on their flags. Are you thinking of a flag you might have seen? Or even a picture of a flag? Something that Mother and Dad might have had around the house somewhere?"

I couldn't think of any flag in our apartment except the two tiny red, white, and blue French flags with toothpick poles that were stuck into the edge of the mirror in Nell and Bibi's room. I felt like a failure. I wanted to give the right answers, but I didn't know what they were.

"I guess I was just thinking of the moon," I admitted finally. "The one up in the sky."

Mr. Burton laughed, two loud barks of laughter that surprised me. "Fair enough," he said. "The moon up in the sky. I shouldn't go around trying to read too much into things, should I?" His teeth were very white against his tanned skin. He stood up and held one square hand out to me. "Mia, thank you so much for helping us out today."

"Are you leaving already?" My voice sounded panicked. I felt my hopes draining away. "But how are you going to find my mom and dad? I didn't tell you anything yet."

"Sure you did," Mr. Burton said. "You gave us a lot to go on. You probably helped us more than you realize."

"My mom knows Red Cross," I said. "And my dad is good at fishing. I know they would do great at living on a desert island if they had to. If they were shipwrecked."

Corporal Pawley stood up from the porch swing. His face was flushed from sitting in the sun. His yellow pencil was tucked behind his ear. "I think you should write that down," I told him, "that part about the island that I just said."

Corporal Pawley looked at Mr. Burton. Mr. Burton nodded. He was still holding my hand in his strong grasp, and I could smell his warm, limy smell. "We'll check into every possibility, Mia," he said. "I give you my word."

Happiness washed though me. My fingertips were tingling. This really was it. The man who could bring my parents back. And I could help him. I took a deep breath, and the Ionia air tasted sweet, rinsed clean of cement dust after the storm.

Kit came to the screen door and peered out. "Would you-all like something cold to drink?" she asked. "Mia bought plenty of Nehis at the store." The way she stood there, smiling at us, hazy behind the screen, made her look mysterious and, suddenly, even beautiful. Her white neck seemed delicate, like a flower stem. I was sure that Mr. Burton must notice it, too. He stepped toward the door where she was standing.

"I was just coming to tell you that Corporal Pawley and I have to be going, Miss Hanks."

Now she should say, "Oh, call me Kit," but she didn't say anything. She stood there smiling her shy smile.

"I have to catch a plane," Mr. Burton said. "But before I go, I want to give you something." He pulled the screen door open slowly, and for just a minute it reminded me of when the groom folds back the bride's veil to kiss her. Kit stepped out onto the porch, blinking in the sunlight. I was sorry to see that she had chewed her lipstick off.

"This is my card," Mr. Burton said. "With my office phone number. It's a direct line. I want you to call anytime you—or Mia—have a question or something to tell me. You can reverse the charges. Okay?" He lifted my aunt's arm, cupping his hand around the edge of her cast. With his other hand he put the card in her palm, and her fingers closed around it. Their heads were almost touching. They stood there.

Behind us, in the still air, a car door clanged shut. Everybody turned around. Dan Flannery was walking toward the house. He was jingling the car keys in his pocket and chewing gum. He slid his sunglasses up to the top of his head and peered at us.

"Hello, hello," he said. "Am I early?"

"No," Kit said. "You're right on time." Her voice sounded faint.

Dan Flannery stepped onto the porch and kissed Kit's cheek with a loud smack. My insides shriveled. Then he leaned down and kissed me on the cheek, a fake kiss, showing off. He'd never kissed me before. I pulled away.

"Dan," Kit said, "this is Mr. Burton and Corporal Pawley. They came out here to talk to Mia."

"Oh," Dan said, "hello there." He acted as if he hadn't noticed until now that two unfamiliar tall men were standing on the porch. "Dan Flannery. Pleasure to meet you." He draped his arm, possessively, across Kit's shoulders.

"He's married," I said out loud.

There was a hush. You could hear the rainwater continuing to drain off the gutters. Dan's arm slid away from my aunt.

"Mia!" Kit whispered. Her face was a deep red.

"Well, folks, I have to catch a plane," Mr. Burton said again. "I will be in touch."

"Yeah, so long now," Corporal Pawley said.

They turned and walked to the car. I stared after them. The Lone Ranger, I thought, and Tonto.

"Mia," Kit said again.

I didn't answer. I didn't have an answer. I felt hard fingers, like pincers, circle my arm. Dan Flannery pulled me around to face them.

"Who the hell do you think you are?" he said in a hard, furious voice. "Huh?"

I tried to pull away, but he tightened his fingers. I felt them press my bone.

"Oww," I yelled.

"Da-yin," Kit said.

"She's going to apologize, Kit! For embarrassing you like that."

"Oh, I don't need—"

"Sure." Dan yanked his hand back off my arm. "She just gets away with it. She's rude and she gets away with it. Huh, Kit?"

I recognized the cold, greedy look on his face. It was just the same as Patsy's when she spooned her soda and kept her sandwich on the plate beside her. They had to own what they saw.

Kit should notice it, too, but she had turned toward me now, fixing me with her anxious gray eyes. "Mia—"

"Aww, your face is a mask of woe," I said.

She opened her mouth and closed it again. She shook her head. "I haven't heard that one in years. Your granny used to use that on me when I was littler than you!"

"Kit!" Dan said.

"Okay, okay." My aunt looked down. "Mia, you were rude, and you should apologize."

They waited. I could hear him suck his breath, ready for the satisfaction of making me say sorry.

"I'm sorry," I said, "but he is married."

Dan Flannery stepped toward me, but I was fast. I dodged past him, in through the screen door. I ran along the dim hallway, through the living room, the kitchen, back to the lonely pine room that felt like the one safe place.

CHAPTER
7

First thing the next morning Kit called up to enroll me in Vacation Bible School at the Church of Christ. It was already done when I wandered into the kitchen to eat breakfast.

"It starts tomorrow morning," Kit said. "It's what you need. To get out of this house more. To spend some time with children your own age. We have to remember to pack you a lunch."

"Bible School?" I repeated, sleepily. My aunt didn't usually talk much in the morning. I stared at the rooster on the cornflakes box. "What's Bible School?"

"Well, it's like camp," Kit said. "Sort of."

Camp. I had always read about it in my books, and I knew that it would be everything I loved to do. Songs around the campfire. Indian lore. Canoe trips. Relay races. I was a good, fast runner, and I pictured myself now, pounding across a stubby Ionia field, while my teammates cheered me on, shouting my name.

"Huh," I said. "Okay, maybe I'll go."

"Oh, you'll go all right," Kit said. "There's not any 'maybe' about it."

I sat back, surprised, waking up now.

"Oh, I know. I've just let you get away with everything. I'm new at this. I've been too soft. But things have to change now." She made a small fist at the end of one cast and thumped it, gingerly, on the table.

I wanted to smile, she was trying so hard.

"After yesterday, your behavior to Dan, well, from now on I'm getting tough." She thumped her fist harder and winced. "Starting right here. With Bible School."

Now I saw. Dan Flannery was somewhere behind this. I wasn't that easy to fool. A shaft of sunlight slanted across the floor. I kicked my sneaker against the table leg. "I don't know," I said finally. "I'm really not supposed to go to Bible places if all they teach is Adam and Eve, stuff like that."

"What?" Kit looked at me blankly.

"Not that there's something *wrong* with Adam and Eve. It's rich in mythology," I said, "but see, that's not enough. They should teach ovulation, too."

"What?" Kit said again, in a faint voice.

"It's for science!" I waved my cereal spoon in the air. "And poetry. You shouldn't stick with just one church. You should be unfettered!"

"Oh, for God's sake!" Kit slammed down her coffee

cup, slopping coffee over the sides. "Unfettered! I bet I know where you got that one."

"I'm not a Communist or anything," I said quickly. I was impressed by her anger, her furious pink face, her shaking hands as she mopped up coffee with her paper napkin.

"Unfettered! That's so typical of Jess!"

I leaned forward, closer to my mom's name, as if I could breathe it in.

"Don't stick with just one church," Kit said, "or one town. Or one life! Just be like the cuckoo bird that flies off and leaves its babies behind." She picked up her coffee cup again, and it rattled on the saucer. The air in the kitchen seemed charged, ready to spark.

My aunt didn't look at me; she stared out the window. "But meanwhile," she said, "*somebody's* got to run the altar guild. *Somebody's* got to run the town. And"—she took a long, deep breath—"somebody's got to feed the baby cuckoos abandoned in that nest."

I dropped my spoon and shoved my bowl across the table at her. "Oh, don't worry," I shouted. "You don't have to feed me anymore. I can find someplace else to go."

I went back to my room and slammed the door behind me. I climbed back under the covers of my bed. There was no sound from the kitchen. I stared at the pine wall and thought of Kit, sitting right on the other side, staring back, already regretting what she'd said to me.

"Abandoned," I repeated, feeling it hurt all over again.

I drew my knees up under my chin, hugging them. The scratches and scabs from climbing palm trees were gone now. My kneecaps were bare and knobby like two old bald heads. My mom could have so many reasons for wanting to go away and leave me. I wasn't smart in school or brave. I never cleaned my fingernails, and so I got pinworms, more than one time. In the nights, when I felt them itching, I cried out until I woke my mom and she had to get up and rub on the ointment. I liked to make her do things for me, things I could have done for myself: cut the bruises out of an apple, run my bathwater, look through the laundry basket for my Girl Scout kerchief. She tied my school shoes every day because I claimed the laces wouldn't stay knotted if I did it. I just stuck one foot onto her lap and then the other, waiting while she picked out the old knots and tugged the laces hard. Bibi and Nell said I wanted to be babied, but it wasn't that. It was how I thought I could keep her there, all for me.

Kit's chair scraped on the kitchen floor, and then there she was, in my doorway. She stood supporting her right elbow with the palm of her left hand. The straps of her nightgown hung on her thin shoulders. "Let's try again," she said.

She came over and sat down on the end of my bed. I hugged my knees harder, looking at her.

"I don't know." She plucked at a corner of the bedspread. "I'm so new at all this."

There was a long silence. It was just the beginning of the day, and already we had worn each other down with fighting. We were both ready to give in. I waited for her to go first.

"So, anyhow," Kit said, "I do understand that you wouldn't want to go against your mother's wishes, but I was thinking about it, and this Vacation Bible School is interdenominational. That means it's many churches all combined together. So that should be okay. It should fit in with your mom's ideas, right?"

The truth, I knew, was that my mom's ideas would never shape themselves around the good points of Bible School or day camp or any kind of group meetings. In Beirut, when had I told her I was signing up to be a Girl Scout, she said, "Oh, honey, think twice. Little beanies. Square knots. All that conformity. Isn't school bad enough?"

But that was exactly what I liked about being a Girl Scout. I loved wearing my uniform every Wednesday and thinking, as I walked to school past the pungent tangerine trees and the Moslem men with red tarbooshes on their heads, that back in the States there were girls like me, wearing uniforms exactly like mine and walking down normal streets with oak trees and square-shaped yards and mailboxes with little metal flags.

And now here I was in a normal town about to walk down one of those normal streets and go to camp. Camp! I tried not to look too jubilant.

"Okay, okay." I sighed. "I'll go."

The Church of Christ was a modern building, an A-frame made of orange bricks. The edges of the roof came down so low on each side that I could rub the rough silver-gray shingles with my fingertips as I followed Kit down a walkway to the yard in back. When we rounded the corner of the building, I stopped still in my tracks. This wasn't camp, certainly not the way I had read about it. There was no lake, no woods, not even a field big enough for relay races. We were at the edge of a black-topped parking lot. Beyond it there was grass and a short chain-link fence. That was all. But what I couldn't take my eyes off were the clusters of kids, standing around in the parking lot and scattered across the rutted, sloping lawn. The way they stood there—shifting from one foot to the other, swinging their lunch boxes, and tipping their jaws up to laugh—was so American. For a minute I thought I couldn't breathe.

"Mia?" Kit had walked on ahead and was turned around, waiting for me.

"Kit!" A tall brown-haired woman wearing a golf skirt broke out of a knot of other mothers and came over to us. She smiled at me. "This must be your little niece I've heard about."

"This is Mia," Kit said. "Mia, this is Mrs. Hilt."

"I've known your aunt—and your mama, too—since we were little girls, littler than you even," Mrs. Hilt said.

I smiled nervously. Looking around, I had just realized that my white ankle socks were wrong. All wrong. The other girls were wearing sneakers with no socks, just bare legs. Even Mrs. Hilt had on sneakers without socks. Her legs were very tan. Below the hem of her yellow golf skirt, her brown, flattened kneecaps looked like two pancakes.

"Speaking of little girls, I want Mia to meet my two, if I can find them." Mrs. Hilt shook her head at Kit and blinked her eyes. "Honest to Pete," she said, "I don't know how I got such little social butterflies. I can't keep up with them. They're always off with their friends, just flying every which way to."

Kit smiled and looked down at me. The corners of my mouth stretched anxiously. My hands were damp. A group of girls about my age skipped past us with their arms linked. They all wore shorts which had been cut from blue jeans with long threads left dangling.

"Corinne!" Mrs. Hilt called out. A tall girl in the middle of the chain turned her head and looked at us. You could tell what she saw: Kit in her big, clumsy casts, me in my glaring ankle socks.

"Come here, sugar," Mrs. Hilt said, motioning with one hand. But Corinne shrugged and was carried off, ponytail bobbing, with the other girls.

"Honest to Pete," Mrs. Hilt said, "I might as well be the wind blowing." She didn't sound mad.

My cheeks burned. I hadn't even officially checked in at Vacation Bible School yet. I could still leave. Kit and I could slip out, back around the church and four short blocks to the house.

"Oh, gosh," Kit said to Mrs. Hilt. "The time. I didn't know it was so late. See you." She led me away, out toward the parking lot. "Lord," she said, "that woman."

"So, are we going back home?" I said.

"Home? No. We're going to go sign you in. At that table over there."

I halted in my tracks.

"Come on," Kit said. "I told you. I'm going to be tough about this."

She continued walking across the parking lot toward the card table that had been set up at the edge of the lawn. I watched her go. She walked with one shoulder cocked from wearing her sling. I didn't know why, but just to look at her, even from the back, you could tell she wasn't one of the moms. An airplane buzzed overhead, but I couldn't see it in the haze. The sun looked like a lightbulb shining through cloth. All around me kids were calling out to one another. Their names—"Debbie!" "Laurie!" "Tom!"—seemed to fly right past me. I stood for a second longer on the hot blacktop, twirling my wilted paper lunch bag, and then I ran, as hard as I could, to catch up with Kit. I figured out, in that second, that if I wasn't with her, I was all by myself.

CHAPTER
8

I was assigned to Group C, the Commandments, and for our first project we had to glue macaroni letters to construction paper to spell out one of the Ten Commandments. I finished before anybody else because I had the shortest one, number eight, THOU SHALT NOT STEAL. Our group leader, Mrs. Wilmott, told us that as we glued the letters in place, we should remember they were God's rules and think to ourselves about how we might obey them better. I thought about the time Jill Pillsworth and I stole the lollipops and smashed them on the swing set. I tried to feel bad about it, but now, sitting here in the heat, I wished I could have one of those lollipops to suck. My mouth was dried out. I remembered the sharp barley sugar smell from the shards of candy, a smell like Hawaiian Punch. I had to have a drink of water. I raised my hand.

"Yes, Mia?" Mrs. Wilmott said my name "My-ah." Everybody stopped gluing and looked up. Most of the girls in Group C seemed younger than I was, and the two who looked as if they could be my age both had something odd about them. One wore braces with a whole assemblage of red headgear, like a harness, and the other one had bushy dark hair that seemed ready to spring right off her head. When I looked at it, I thought of the word *lava*.

"Could I go get a drink of water?"

"Well," Mrs. Wilmott said, "as soon as one of the other girls is finished with her work, the two of you can go. Remember, we want to do things by the buddy system."

I sat, waiting, peeling strips of glue off my fingertips. Across the yard, at another group of tables, I could see Corinne Hilt and her dress-alike friends. They were Group D, the Devotions. I couldn't tell what kind of project they were working on, but some of them seemed to be holding paintbrushes. They were talking and jumping around and leaning across the tables, stretching their tanned arms to point at things. Most of them wore several bangle bracelets that sparkled on their wrists. I turned back toward the Commandments, hunched over their macaroni letters, and I knew: I was in with the losers.

I sighed, and Mrs. Wilmott gave me a bashful smile. She tried to be nice, but she was the type of leader they pick for losers. Somebody almost pretty, but there's something wrong. With Mrs. Wilmott, it was that she was so tall and thin and her hands were big as a man's. Her blue plaid skirt hung off her hips, and her blouse never stayed tucked in. Mr. Wilmott was the leader of Group A, the boys' group, and every so often he wandered over to check on what we were doing. "How goes it, Mrs. Wilmott?" he asked each time. He was tall, too, with a lazy eye that slid to one side, not looking at you. They were newlyweds, Mrs. Wilmott told us shyly, and he was studying to be a pastor. She smoothed her messy blouse with her big, bony hands every time he came by.

Now she motioned to me and said, "I see that Sinclair Smith has finished her work, so you two can go off to the girls' room if you want."

Sinclair Smith turned out to be the girl with the bushy hair. She had completed her commandment, number two, THOU SHALT NOT MAKE ANY GRAVEN IMAGE, but when she handed it in, Mrs. Wilmott said, "Oh, dear, I'm afraid there's only supposed to be one *M* in the word *image*."

"Oops," Sinclair said. She took the paper back from Mrs. Wilmott and flicked off the extra letter with one fingernail.

"Okay," she said to me. "Let's go."

We set off across the yard toward the cinder-block building that adjoined the church. Sinclair walked lazily, skidding the toes of her sneakers through the grass. She yawned and languidly pushed her wild hair off the back of her neck. Her hair looked more than ever like something that might erupt, but everything else about her seemed slow motion.

* * *

In the girls' room, first thing, I went into a toilet stall and took off my ankle socks. They were damp and stretched out. When I held them up, they sagged, like feet with no bones. Now that I had them off, I couldn't think where to put them. A toilet flushed, and a stall door squeaked. I could see Sinclair's sneakers shuffling across the floor toward the row of sinks. She would probably be waiting right there until I came out since she couldn't go back to Group C without me. I wadded the socks up in my fists. I sat there. It didn't seem like a good idea to throw them into the toilet. But if I carried them out of the stall to put them in the trash barrel, Sinclair would see. Finally, looking around, I figured out that if I stood on the toilet seat, I could pitch them, one at a time, onto the top of the big porcelain water tank that was mounted overhead. Then I flushed the toilet for sound effects and went out.

Sinclair was sitting on the edge of one sink, facing me. "Sheesh," she said, "I thought you fell in." She laced her fingers together and stretched her arms until her knuckles popped. "So, what happened to your socks?" she asked.

In the mirror I saw my face turn pink. I shrugged. "I took them off. They were too hot."

I walked to a sink and began running water. I leaned over and cupped my hands to get a drink. The bathroom smelled so strongly of Pine Sol that the water tasted of it, too.

"There's a drinking fountain out yonder in the hall," Sinclair said.

"I like to drink this way, if you don't mind." I scooped up another handful of water and made slurping sounds to demonstrate how much I was enjoying it. It felt good on my burning face.

"How did your mother break her arms?" Sinclair asked. For someone who walked around with her eyes half shut, she seemed to notice everything.

"That's my aunt," I said. "Not that it's any of your business."

"Okay, how did your *aunt* break her arms?"

"An accident."

"Naw," Sinclair said, swinging her legs idly from her perch on the sink. "And I thought she did it on purpose."

I spun around to face her. "Okay. Fine. If you have to know everything. If you like being the nosy type. Fine. I'll tell you so you can quit bothering me. I broke my aunt's arms. She was trying to catch me when I jumped from someplace high. Okay?"

Sinclair's drowsy eyes opened wide. They were a surprising deep, inky blue. "Hey," she said slowly, figuring it out, "were you that one on the water tower? That got written up in the newspaper?"

I nodded.

"That was you!"

"Yes." I bowed my head, wanting to smile now, that feeling you get when you tell bad news.

"Sheesh, that was wonderful," Sinclair said. "What you did. Jumping."

I looked up. She was looking right back at me, rapt, with those deep, shining eyes.

"Were you afraid?" she asked.

I shrugged. "No. I don't know. I didn't think about it. I just did it."

"Aha," Sinclair said. "Virtue is bold!"

I reached for a paper towel to dry my hands. I seemed to have her admiration, but I didn't know what to do with it. It was time to go back to join the rest of the camp, but Sinclair wasn't stirring from her throne on the sink. She sat there, swinging her legs.

"And your parents," she said suddenly. "They're missing at sea?"

"Why don't you just shut up?" I said. She stopped swinging her legs. "You don't even know." My voice was starting to break. "It's none of your beeswax where they are."

I marched over to the bathroom door.

"Sheesh," Sinclair said behind me. She slid down from the sink. I heard her feet thump onto the floor, but I didn't slow down to wait for her.

Outside, the sun seemed dazzlingly bright. I walked across the grass, blinking. Sinclair trailed a couple of yards behind me. We didn't talk. Group D had finished their project, and as I passed their tables, they were tacking it up, a big banner painted in bold pink and orange that said: THE DEVOTIONS. It wasn't fair, I thought bitterly.

Even their name sounded great, like the name of a rock and roll band.

Back at our own tables Mrs. Wilmott had collected the finished macaroni commandments and was arranging them in order. When I looked down at the squares of construction paper, I saw that mine was the only one with evenly spaced letters, the only one not splotched with glue.

"That's too bad, isn't it?" I said in a low voice to Mrs. Wilmott.

"What is, dear?" She seemed honestly not to know. In Beirut my teacher would have rejected all those sloppy efforts. She would have stamped them CARELESS WORK.

"Well." I pointed to the glue spots, the slanting letters. The gap in Sinclair's word *IM AGE* looked laughable, like when you blacked out somebody's tooth in a photograph. "It's too bad not everybody did a good job. They didn't do their best."

"Oh, My-ah." Mrs. Wilmott squatted down next to me. Her knees shot forward, stretching her skirt fabric. She put her arm on my shoulders, and I could smell her skin, a bland, hidden smell like mushrooms. "My-ah," she repeated. Her tone was sad. "We must never pass judgment on the good efforts of our neighbors. It's not our place, is it? Only God can really know what's in our hearts and what makes us do the work we do."

I looked back at the worktable, confused. I never thought of outguessing God. I just didn't want to be laughed at when the Devotions saw our sloppy project. I was in the wrong group.

"Do we have a little problem here, Mrs. Wilmott?" Mr. Wilmott stood staring down at us. Mrs. Wilmott shook her head. Her arm was still around me. I couldn't help it, I pictured them together, their long, clumsy bodies, his sliding eye.

"My-ah and I just shared a good little lesson about how we need to treat our neighbors."

"Aha," Mr. Wilmott said. He towered over us. "Well, love thy neighbor as thyself," he said. "I know it's not always easy, but it's what the Lord asks of us, My-ah."

I watched the girls from my group sitting down to open their lunch boxes under two nearby oak trees. The girl who wore the headgear had unstrapped it, and it sat in the grass beside her, like a pet. I looked at the Wilmotts. They smiled back at me. They were in with the losers. You couldn't just tell them.

"Okay," I said. "Well, I think I'll eat lunch now."

"And, My-ah"—Mr. Wilmott wagged one finger at me—"I know you'll look for the neighborly love that's in your heart, won't you?"

Mrs. Wilmott stood up, and her knees cracked. She smiled her bashful smile. Mr. Wilmott put his arm around her. When they looked down at me, they seemed like giraffes, big but so easy to topple. I wasn't going to hurt their feelings.

"Sure," I lied. "I will."

At lunch nobody talked to me. I had seated myself a little apart from the Commandments, on the fringe of the Devotions, and I could hear parts of the conversation from both groups, but it was full of names and places I didn't know, like a secret code: "Karen Cloud passed a love note to Mike Bost at HI-Y." "Jody said her mama is taking her to Tullahoma this Friday."

I sat in the shade of overlapping branches from two big oak trees, and whenever the breeze stirred the leaves, sunlight strobed across my legs and then vanished. After I'd finished my sandwich and folded up the wax paper, I sat alone, splintering the pieces of old, soft acorns with my thumbnail, trying to look occupied.

"Want some Good and Plentys?"

I looked up. Sinclair was standing there. She shook the cardboard package to make the candy rattle.

"Okay," I said. "Sure." I didn't like Good & Plentys, but she was somebody to talk to.

"Hold out your hand." Sinclair dropped down beside me and poured candy into my cupped palm.

"Okay," I said. "Save some for yourself."

The tree branches rustled above us, and sunlight flicked across Sinclair's wild hair, looking, for a second, like shooting flames.

"Your hair makes me think of a volcano," I blurted.

Sinclair looked at me.

"Well, maybe more of a lava flow. In school they

showed a filmstrip of lava flow. They're wild, but beautiful, kind of."

"Yeah." Sinclair popped a pink Good & Plenty into her mouth. "I saw one. In Hawaii one time." She smoothed back her hair with her sticky fingers. It poked out crazily on top of her head. "Thanks," she added.

Next to us a group of Devotions had started doing cheerleading routines. They chanted and cartwheeled. Sunlight flashed across their legs as they high-kicked, showing off. The grass where I was sitting, underneath the trees, was short and soft, almost like moss. I rubbed one hand, back and forth, across it. I had a desperate feeling, watching the Devotions' sneakers lifting, lifting, toes pointed, in unison. If I didn't get to be friends with them, I could never be happy again.

"Want to come over sometime?" Sinclair spoke up suddenly.

"What?" I said. I figured that Corinne Hilt must be the Devotions' leader. She wasn't performing the cheer herself, but sitting cross-legged, watching.

"I think your jumps were good," she told the others, "but your splits were kind of high." She reached back and twisted her ponytail to make it curl.

"To my house," Sinclair said. "Want to come over sometime?"

"Oh," I said. "Sure." I found another acorn by my feet and speared it with my thumbnail. Two members of the Devotions were running across the blacktop, coming from the back of the church. One of them was almost plump. Her legs made a rubbing noise as she ran.

"You-all won't believe what happened in the rest room!" She was out of breath. "Tell them, Cathy!"

"Well," the other girl said. She was the one who'd had her arm linked with Corinne's in the morning. "I was sitting there on the you-know-what, and all of a sudden this white cloth thing dropped down from the ceiling, from out of nowhere. It fell right on me. I screamed bloody murder."

"It was some old putrefied sock!" the plump girl said.

I couldn't move. I couldn't look at Sinclair next to me. I tried to swallow, but my tongue sat, flat and heavy, like a disk in my mouth.

"I had to wash my leg off where it brushed against me." Cathy pursed her lips in disgust. "My mama says you get scabies from things like that."

"You do," another Devotion said. "Or something worse."

A breeze rustled the oak leaves overhead. It sounded like somebody whispering, "Please."

"But the thing is," the plump girl said, "we were the only ones in the rest room. So, where did the sock come from? This stinky sock! It couldn't just drop out of the ceiling by itself."

"I mean," Cathy said, "whose is it?"

"I think I know," Sinclair said. The Devotions all turned to look at her.

I thought of what I could do: stand up and run out of Bible School or pretend to faint. I sat, frozen, staring into the parking lot at what appeared to be a small dark pond, shimmering in the middle of the asphalt. It was a trick of the heat, I knew. If you tried to walk toward it, the water would disappear.

"You-all weren't really alone in there," Sinclair said. "Someone was with you. Sending you a message."

"On the commode?" Cathy said in a shocked voice.

"Someone was trying to communicate." Sinclair continued. "Some spirit."

The Devotions looked at one another.

"I'm getting goose bumps," the plump one said. "Look."

"In a church bathroom," another one said. "It might have been the Holy Spirit!"

Corinne Hilt shot a long look in our direction. "Whatever it was," she said finally, "I think we should report the whole thing to Mrs. Carter." She hooked out her elbows, and girls linked up from both sides. They marched off in a line.

I took a deep breath. My eyes ached from staring straight ahead, without blinking, for so long. A whistle blew. It meant lunchtime was over. I stood up and brushed twigs and pieces of acorn off the backs of my legs. My hands were icy. Sinclair tilted the candy box up to her mouth and tapped on the end. She stood up and yawned, a blast of licorice fumes.

"How about tomorrow?" she said as we walked back

toward the Commandments' table. "You could ask your aunt if you can come to my house after Bible School." Her voice was sleepy and careless, as if it didn't matter whether I came or not.

"Okay." I tried to sound as offhand as she did.

We cut through the parking lot. If you wanted to, I thought, you could consider it a miracle that we were walking on the very spot that the dark pond had covered, just moments before.

CHAPTER

9

Sinclair's house was red brick with a pair of big fluted columns in front. It was set back on a half circle driveway, and the boxwood bushes were clipped into cylinders with flat tops. I followed Sinclair across the lawn. I felt shy suddenly. She must be rich, even though she didn't seem like a rich person with her messy nest of hair and her droopy posture. I watched her skim her hand idly across the sheared crown of a boxwood as we passed by. The grass beneath our feet was green and perfect, like cellophane.

Inside, it was cooler and the light was dim. I blinked a few times so I could see better. All along one side of the house, wooden shutters were closed, keeping out the heat. I had never known of people who used their shutters before.

"Want a milk shake?" Sinclair said. She led the way

down a long, wide corridor that smelled like floor wax. On either side I glimpsed into high-ceilinged rooms with dark furniture and big paintings on the walls.

"They don't let me drink Cokes," Sinclair said, "because I get too many cavities. But I can have all the milk shakes I want." She snapped on the lights in the kitchen. There was no sign of any grown-up around. For a minute I wondered if this was really Sinclair's house at all. Maybe she knew this place would be empty and brought me here for a joke. Or maybe her mother worked here as a maid or a cook.

"Where's your mom?" I said.

Sinclair shrugged. "Probably riding. That's where she usually is."

"She's a writer?"

Sinclair made a hooting noise. "I said *riding*. On a horse. Giddyup."

"Oh." I looked around the kitchen. Everything was oversize and chrome colored. Sinclair opened the door of an enormous freezer and started pulling out cartons of ice cream.

"Strawberry," she said, "or chocolate or peach?"

"I don't care." I felt shy, but I didn't want to show it. Sinclair was rich. Her mom was out riding a horse. Everything was different from what I'd thought. I had to get used to it. A ceiling fan revolved overhead. Through a doorway I could see a pantry with bushel baskets of onions and potatoes.

"How many are in your family?" I asked.

"Five." Sinclair was dumping scoops of pink ice cream into the glass container of a large blender. "My mama and my daddy. Me. And my two brothers. But Marshall, my oldest brother, goes to college, so he's not here that much."

All of this for five people! I stuck my hands into the pockets of my shorts and tried not to look awed.

"Presto chango!" Sinclair flipped up the switch on the blender, and we watched the scoops of ice cream jolt up to the lid and fly apart.

"Where I really wanted to go was Catholic Bible Camp," Sinclair said, sighing, "but my parents said no."

"How come?"

We were sitting on the rug in Sinclair's room. It was a powder blue rug, very thick. You could draw pictures in the nap with your index finger. Our milk shakes were finished, and we were eating grapes, spitting the seeds into our cupped hands.

"Because we're not Roman Catholic. But I might convert when I'm sixteen," Sinclair said. Her eyes opened wide, almost purple in her long white face. Here, in her big, cool house, she looked different, almost pretty, unlike at Bible School, where the heat made her damp shirt cling to her bony shoulders and frizzed her hair in all directions.

"We're supposed to be Methodist," she added, "but that's a laugh. We never go to church except on Christmas Eve."

I bit into a grape seed, and its bitter taste hung in my

mouth. Next, she would ask what religion I was and I would have to answer something. I stared at the bars of light that came in through the shutters. I was ready to lie, to keep it simple. I thought of the word *Episcopal.* To me it always sounded embarrassing, like the name of a body part, and now that seemed good—convincing, not something you would make up about yourself.

But Sinclair didn't ask the question. Instead she leaned back, resting on her elbows, and talked on, as if I had asked her a question.

"The way I decided I should be Catholic is from reading this book about saints. Catholics have all the good saints. Like St. Bernadette and Joan of Arc and St. Clare of Assisi. I mean, if you're Methodist, you don't get all those saints."

"Oh." The only thing I thought about saints was that they wore dull gold halos in old paintings, nothing exciting. Sinclair sat forward suddenly. The points of her elbows left two dents in the blue rug, she was so bony.

"See," she said, "everybody thinks saints are just goody-goodies, but that's all wrong. They were adventurous and wild even. People thought they were crazy sometimes or doing evil things, but everything they did turned out to be right." She jumped up and tossed her grape seeds into the wastebasket. They made a pinging sound, like BBs, hitting the metal. "I'll show you what I'm talking about."

She crossed the room and pulled open a bureau drawer. She wasn't moving her usual lazy way, almost sleepwalking. Clothes fell out of the drawer as she rummaged through it, but she didn't stop to pick them up. In a minute she pulled out a small green book and carried it over to me.

"Go ahead," she said. "You can see for yourself."

It was called *The Bedside Book of Saints*. I flipped the pages while Sinclair looked over my shoulder. The illustrations were in thin, muddy colors, like the pictures in an arithmetic textbook, and the writing was tiny. I didn't read the descriptions, but I studied each drawing so Sinclair would know I was paying attention. She was right about the saints being adventurous. They rode horses, brandished swords, and climbed mountains, carrying small children on their backs. Halfway through the book there was a picture of a dark-haired girl in a bride's dress, running through the woods. Her veil streamed out behind her.

"There!" Sinclair said. "That's St. Clare, the one I was talking about before. She's running off to meet St. Francis."

"Are they getting married?"

"No." Sinclair shook her head slowly. She had a small, faraway smile on her face.

"So how come she's wearing a wedding dress then?" I was annoyed by Sinclair's calm smile. It was like the girl in the picture.

"Because." She gave a deep sigh. "She's showing that she's changing her life. When she gets to St. Francis, he cuts her hair short and she puts on a sackcloth dress. They spend the rest of their lives helping people."

"What's so adventurous about that?"

Sinclair scooped the hair off the back of her neck and bunched it on top of her head like a plume. "I don't know," she said. "I just like it." She let her hair drop. "Anyhow," she said, "my name means St. Clare. Sinclair. St. Clare."

I looked at her and then back at the pictures in the book. She really wanted to be like a saint. I flipped a few more pages. I was getting interested now, in spite of the dingy drawings and the small print. It was something about Sinclair herself. She acted so careless about everything, except that she picked out this one thing to care about. That made it seem real.

"I wouldn't show this book to everybody," Sinclair said, "but I especially wanted to show it to you."

"Oh. Thanks." I was transfixed by a grisly picture of St. Justina with a sword piercing her throat.

"Want to know why?"

"Okay." I flipped the pages. The more pictures you looked at, the more tortures there were. Spikes. Flames. Beheadings.

"Because I think you might be one. A saint."

I slammed the book shut. "Why?" I breathed.

"You know. The water tower. How you jumped, like something told you to do it."

"So?" My heart raced. This was too close. There were

things nobody should know. The orders that came from the air had too much power. You could never just say them out loud.

"See, that's the way it happens. The saints do stuff like climbing high turrets or going out to fight dragons because something tells them to do it, even if they don't know who or what. Sometimes it's a miracle, and no one knows it until later. It's all in the book. You can take it home and read it."

"No, thanks." I dropped the book onto the rug. I didn't want to see more. It was like having pinworms and looking at the illustration in Nell's medical dictionary. It made the itching worse, knowing that was inside you. Now this, a saint! Always, all I'd wanted was just to be like anybody else, just regular.

There was a tap on the door, and a woman's voice said, "Sinclair?"

Sinclair extended one leg and used her bare toes to nudge the bowl of grapes out of sight, under the bed. "We're not allowed to bring food upstairs," she whispered. "It might attract mice."

"Sinclair," the voice said again.

"Come on in, Mama."

The door opened, and there was her mother, the rider. I first saw her tall boots. She wore jeans and a plain pink shirt with the sleeves rolled up. Her hair was wild, like Sinclair's, but tied back. She was beautiful; she had a nice horsey smell.

"This is Mia," Sinclair said, "the one I told you about."

"Hello, Mia."

"Hi." I sat there shyly. I couldn't shake hands; my right fist was filled with grape pits.

"What are you girls up to?" There was a sound in her voice, something tender and nosy together, that mothers use. I felt the sadness start, a familiar ache in my chestbone.

"Oh, just stuff," Sinclair said. "Homework."

"Homework?" her mother said. "It's summertime!"

"Yeah, well, this is homework for Bible School." Sinclair grabbed the book and held it up. "See."

The Bedside Book of Saints," her mother read, squinting. "Ugh, I don't think they ought to be giving you work to do. You're supposed to have *fun* in the summer."

"I know," Sinclair said, sighing heavily.

"Well, I might just have a word with that Mrs. Carter or whoever is handing out homework over there."

"Good," Sinclair said, "because it's really too much work. Right, Mia?"

I had a wide, shocked grin. I couldn't talk. If you had a mom, standing right there, only wishing good things for you, you shouldn't just tell lies to her so easily.

"Well," Sinclair's mother said, "I'm going to take a shower. Don't you-all work too hard." She stepped back and closed the door behind her.

"Sinclair!" I said in a furious voice.

"Oh, don't worry." Sinclair was picking at something

inside the back cover of the saints book. "She won't talk to anybody at Bible School. She always says stuff like that and then she just forgets."

"But, Sinclair—"

"There!" Sinclair extracted a paper pocket containing a library card from the back of the book. IONIA FREE LIBRARY was printed across the top. "I didn't even have to rip the paper."

"That's a library book?"

"It was," Sinclair said. "Now it's mine."

"You took it."

"Yeah." Sinclair shrugged. "If you sign it out, you have to give it back in two weeks. I needed it for longer."

There was another knock on the door, and Sinclair's mom stuck her head back in. "Mia, if you'd like to stay for dinner, you're welcome. We're going to barbecue."

"Yeah, stay," Sinclair said. "We can call your aunt."

More than anything, I wanted to stay. I wanted to get away from another night of Dan Flannery and his sacks of hamburgers and my aunt giving him everything, as if he were king. I wanted to eat dinner with a family, around a big table, with the dad cutting the meat—I pictured Sinclair's dad, handsome, important, the light catching on his gold cuff links when he held the carving knife— and the mom saying, "Put your napkin in your lap," in the voice that meant somebody was taking care of you.

But before I could say yes, I already knew the order

was coming. The more you wanted something, the more likely it was that you would have to give it up.

"I can't!" I said miserably. "I mean, I have to go home."

Sinclair walked with me, back toward Kit's so I wouldn't get lost. A hot breeze was blowing, and the air smelled sharp as it ruffled the tops of the boxwood bushes and scattered the browning magnolia petals from high in the trees. Sinclair kicked a flat stone slowly ahead of her, down the sidewalk. At the corner, she knocked it sideways into the storm drain. It clattered at the bottom, no splash. Everything was dry.

"So," Sinclair said, "do you have to cook dinner since your aunt has those broken arms?"

"No. We eat these greasy hamburgers that her boyfriend brings. Every night."

"Your aunt has a boyfriend? Is he cute?"

"He's married!" I said. "And he has these little eyes that look at you like he can take anything he wants. Anyhow, he hates me, too. I don't care."

"He's married?" Sinclair had started kicking a new stone, but now she stopped. She looked interested. "And your aunt is his girlfriend?"

I nodded.

"Wow," Sinclair said. Her inky eyes shone. "That's adultery, you know, like in the Ten Commandments!" She lowered her voice. "So, do you ever hear them doing it?"

"Doing what?"

"You know." Sinclair looked at me. "Don't you know?"

Then I did know. I blushed so hard I could feel the roots of my hair prickle. "They don't do *that*," I said.

Sinclair was silent.

"I mean, maybe they kiss sometimes, but that's all."

Sinclair just looked at me.

"But Sinclair," I said, "she has two broken arms!"

Sinclair rolled her eyes. She nudged at her stone with the toe of her shoe.

"Listen, I know the way home from here," I told her, walking on. "You don't have to come with me. You can just go on back home. Go ahead."

"Wait." She looked up. "I wanted to ask you. Want to start a club with me? A saints club?"

The saints again. "No."

"Come on. We could have rules and meetings and a secret handshake. All that club stuff."

"I don't know." I couldn't forget those saints in the book, their faces rapturous while they were being stabbed or burning up in flames for following their orders. But maybe a club would be good, making it all seem normal, just something kids did. "Could we have a secret code too, maybe?"

"Sure." Sinclair waved one hand toward the sky. "We can do anything we want."

"Well, okay. A club."

"Okay!" Sinclair smiled her slow, dazzling smile. The

late sunlight caught in the tips of her crazy hair. She stole and lied to her mom and probably did everything Mrs. Wilmott's macaroni rules said not to do. But Mrs. Wilmott didn't know this: If you had to pick which way to go, you'd follow Sinclair every time.

CHAPTER
10

I took Mr. Burton's card from Kit's bureau and telephoned his office number. A woman answered, "Middle East."

"Is that Mr. Burton's office?" I whispered.

"Yes, it is. Who's calling, please?"

I hung up, thrilled. It was enough for now. His office in Washington, D.C., really existed, there at the end of the telephone line.

Kit came in from the porch with the mail. "Something for you," she said, "a postcard."

It was from Bibi, a beach scene from Cape Cod. They had visited an artist colony there and a sculptor with a black goatee had asked her to stay and pose for a bust of Athena, but her dad said no, they had to drive up to Plymouth Rock.

"Pallas Athena!" Bibi wrote. "Goddess of wisdom and art! I had no taste for ersatz Pilgrims after that. I stayed in the car and wrote a poem."

"What does that mean?" I held the card out to Kit with my finger under the word *ersatz*.

"Well, it means artificial," she said, smiling. "But what the whole thing really means is that Bibi didn't get her way, so she sat in the car and sulked instead of seeing Plymouth Rock."

Kit was up early most mornings now. She made instant coffee and toast and sat at the kitchen table. When I woke up, the first thing I usually heard was the clink of her spoon, stirring the coffee.

"Teenagers go in for that kind of thing," she said, "sulking and writing poetry." She lifted her right arm and thumped the cast against her chest. "High drama."

"Did you used to do that? Write poems and stuff?"

Kit turned Bibi's postcard over and studied the picture: three seagulls on the pale sand. She shook her head. When she squinted, there were two fine lines at the edges of her gray eyes. She wasn't old, she was younger than my mom, but it was still hard to picture her as a teenager, hard to think of what she'd call fun.

"Well," Kit said, "huh. When I was a teenager, I reckon I didn't have much time to feel sorry for myself. I had a widowed mother, and Jess, your mom, was already gone. So everything was up to me. I got good grades. I played basketball. I stitched the best quilted potholders in home ec. I was way too busy to write a poem!"

She smiled, making the creases show again, next to her eyes. Her elbows were resting on the table, and both arms in their casts were extended in front of her. "But now"—she held up the casts—"I suppose I have plenty of time."

That was true. I thought of how she sat in the mornings, stirring her coffee until the sunlight spread across the table and reached the other end of the room. When we first arrived from Beirut, she had always been in a rush, ironing a skirt, curling her hair, dashing off to her job. Now I was the one with someplace to go, with things to get done. I still had to get dressed and pack a lunch before Bible School. I stood up.

The light coming through the gauzy curtains looked almost the same as the butter sliding across the toast. Kit sat there. She pushed her spoon back and forth between her fingers. Her face was smooth, relaxed. "I guess it looks like I just sit here," she said. "But you know what? I'm really sulking. I'm making up for lost time."

In Tennessee the kids said "soft drink" for "soda pop" and "tennis shoe" for "sneaker." The Ionia streetlights looked like ice-cube trays instead of the lozenge shape we'd had in Ohio. I remembered Nell telling me, "There's America and there's America, as you will learn." But so far that still wasn't true. The differences weren't that big. Every day at Bible School, when I sat on the edge of the blacktop, the kids pulled white, square sandwiches from their lunch sacks. It was a million miles from Beirut, where you bought bread from a vendor who balanced the stack of loaves on his head and the children drank *liban*, their buttermilk, from the copper pails they carried with them. The kids around me couldn't even guess. I watched them chew their Moon Pies and wad up the wrappers. They never had to think twice about what was home.

Sinclair and I used lunchtimes to work on our club. We argued over the choices. Sinclair wanted purple and red for our official colors, but I held out for blue and gold. Finally we reached a compromise: purple and gold. Her plan was for us to take turns reading episodes in the saints book and report on them at our lunchtime meetings, but I refused. I already knew all I had to know about what it was like, a saint's life. It wasn't really a voice that told you what to do. It was words; they were just there. You did what they said. In the past few nights, when I woke up thirsty, and the whole house was dark and quiet, I knew I had to go into the kitchen and slowly touch each number on the face of the luminous clock, even though I was terrified by the stillness and the clock's steady blue glow.

In the daylight none of that seemed real. I wasn't any saint. I sat eating baloney with mustard and plucking at the blunt, dry grass at the edge of the parking lot. Sinclair and I were trying to work out a secret signal we could use to alert each other when we had urgent club business to discuss.

"How about if we just say something like 'Jack and Jill went up the hill'?" I suggested.

"Nah, not a *nursery* rhyme," Sinclair said. "What does that have to do with saints or anything?"

I was getting annoyed. She had already been the one to choose our motto, "Virtue Is Bold," and our emergency meeting spot, an alcove that led to the service door of the church.

"I know," she said now. "How about 'My cousin Clare is visiting me'? *Clare.* Get it?"

"Ick," I said. "It sounds like one of those things people say for getting your period."

"It does not!" Sinclair said. "Sheesh." She tore open a small bag of Fritos from her lunch. "What they say for that," she said, chewing noisily, "is 'Mia fell off the roof' or 'Mia has the curse.'"

"Why are you using *my* name? I said. "Use your own name." The salty Fritos smell made my mouth water.

"Here." Sinclair held out the bag. She was always generous, even in the middle of an argument. "Okay," she said, "we'll compromise then. Our signal can be 'My cousin Clare fell off the roof.'"

"Ha-ha-ha," I said.

"No. Wait, I've got it: Mrs. Wilmott fell off the roof!"

"Sinclair!"

I looked around, but nobody was paying attention to us. After a few days of camp, patterns had been formed. Everybody had a place. The Devotions practiced their cheers under the tree. The boys ate lunch quickly, in a group, farther up the parking lot and then spent the rest of the time dribbling two basketballs and elbowing one another out of the way. Both basketballs needed air, and they hit the pavement with a hard, final sound. You could feel the thud in your chest each time.

The other girls from our group crouched down in a circle, playing jacks, with the exception of the girl with the headgear. She sat by herself every day, reading a white leather Bible that she carried with her. The edges of the pages were gilt. Her name was Lady-Anne, and she was named after a hunting dog of her dad's. Sinclair knew that because her parents were friends with Lady-Anne's parents.

The whistle blew for the end of lunch. I saw Mrs. Wilmott walking over, through the parking lot, coming to collect us. She would clap her big hands once and say, "Oh, Commandments," in her uncertain voice, and we would have to line up, branded as members of the inferior group, while the Devotions stood by, golden and poised, waiting for their own leader, Jeannie.

Jeannie was the opposite of Mrs. Wilmott in every way. Small and round-faced, she dressed in pink Bermuda shorts or chopped-off jeans, like an older version of the Devotions themselves. She strummed a guitar when they sang hymns, while Mrs. Wilmott could only lead us with a single bleating tone on her pitch pipe. It was okay, having a club, being a saint with Sinclair, but after lunch you had to face the fact that you were a Commandment again.

"Hey, I know," Sinclair said. "I just thought of what our code phrase should be. For real, I mean."

"Wait," I said. "I thought of one, too." I hadn't. I just wanted to win.

"Mine is 'The lilies are blooming,' " Sinclair said, "because it said in the book a lily is a symbol for St. Clare."

"Oh, so now it gets to just be about *your* name," I said.

"Fine." Sinclair sighed. "*You* pick it then. What did you think of?"

Nothing. My mind was blank. I pressed down on the soft tar, making a round dent with the toe of my sneaker. Tennis shoe.

"Well?"

" 'O beautiful for spacious skies.' " It was what I could come up with then, a song about America.

Sinclair rolled her eyes.

"Well, you said *I* could pick it."

"Fine," Sinclair said. " 'O beautiful for spacious skies.' "

"Fine." I was the winner.

In the late afternoon Mrs. Swope came out in her yard to work. She pruned the bushes herself, holding the big shears high over her head, like crossed swords. She peered at each branch for a long time and then attacked, snipping. Her hands shook.

"I hired me a boy to do this last summer," she told me, "but he never could do right. He left long snags above the buds, and that's just the way a canker gets in."

When she reached up to cut, the tops of her stockings were revealed, rolled at her knees. I had come over with the idea of offering to help, but now I wouldn't dare. I might let in a canker or something worse.

The breeze usually came up at the end of the day, but it was a warm, heavy breeze, like breath. It didn't cool you off. I heard the whining sound that meant they had just turned off the machinery at the cement plant. It was winding down. You got so used to the buzz it made that you didn't notice until it stopped.

"Next, I'm going after these weeds," Mrs. Swope said. "They'll be the ruination of you if you don't get them first." She pointed with the shears. "That there is burdock." Her mouth bunched as if she had tasted something bad. "And this one, with the purple, that's joe-pye weed."

It had never crossed my mind that weeds had separate names and that someone might know them. But it was like the information my dad always had. If you blew bubbles in your milk with a straw, he would explain to you why it worked: surface tension. And if you walked with him down the Corniche and saw the men with their tarbooshes on their heads, he would tell about Moslems, what they believed, who their rulers were. Caliph, emir, sultan, sheik. The titles rolled off his tongue.

"I could help you with the weeds," I said to Mrs. Swope. "I could pull them out." I stared down. I didn't want to see if she was wearing that kindly look that grown-ups had before they told you no.

"Well, these are tough ones," Mrs. Swope said. "You'd have to dig them out. And get all the root." The way she said it, it rhymed with *foot*. "You want to try that?"

I nodded.

"All right then, get the little spade out of the tool basket that's over yonder."

We worked then, not talking much. Mrs. Swope reached up into the branches, and I bent down, digging into the dense red dirt. We were a team, just as if we'd practiced it. The shears snipped overhead, and every so often little clippings dropped down my neck, tickling like a haircut.

Each time I reached the end of a white, fleshy burdock root and yanked it out, it seemed like the best thing I had ever done, and I forgot everything except the steady heat, the snip of the shears, and the spade cutting into the earth. It could just go on and on.

A car drove down the street too fast, skittering gravel as it braked. Mrs. Swope and I looked up. It was Dan Flannery's blue car, swinging into Kit's driveway. Mrs. Swope watched for a minute, and when she turned back, her mouth was bunched, the same way it had been before she said "joe-pye weed."

We went back to our work, not saying anything. I didn't look across the road anymore, but I heard the car door close, and I knew that he was carrying in the hamburger sacks, that the evening routine was about to begin all over again. I pushed the spade down hard with my foot into the solid red dirt. You could study dirt, but it wasn't like the sand on the beach, particles, a thousand different sizes and shapes. It didn't seem to hold any clues to where it came from.

After a while I heard the screen door squeak, and Kit called to me that it was time to eat supper.

"Just a minute," I told her. She shut the door, and I kept digging, going for one more root. Mrs. Swope put her hand on my shoulder and let it rest there.

"Just one more root," I said. I was out of breath. My fingers were stiff from gripping the shovel. I hadn't felt so good for a long, long time.

"Mia."

I stopped, and this time I saw it on her face. She was saying no. "Run along now, honey. They're waiting on you." She took my shovel. "You don't want to get us both in a pickle."

After we ate hamburgers, Dan Flannery pulled a toothpick out of his pants pocket and chewed on the end.

"The Tullahoma people signed on the line today," he said, "so I'm looking at a pretty good bonus."

"Da-yin," Kit said, "congratulations."

"What's dirt made out of?" I said.

Dan Flannery turned his head slowly in my direction. "What kind of question is that?" he said.

It was the kind of question you would say in my family and they would all want to tell you, everything, about rocks and mold and the depth of the ocean, about how the whole world was made. Just one question would lead to that, all their voices talking over one another, spilling out words or even whole stories of volcanoes and the dust on the moon until you couldn't listen anymore. Only now I would have.

"I'm speaking to you." Dan Flannery narrowed his eyes.

"Oh, well," Kit said, "she's just—"

"No!" Dan Flannery held up one hand for silence. "I'm speaking to her now, and I expect her to answer, like a civilized person." The toothpick bobbled in his mouth.

"See, I was digging today, in the dirt," I began.

"Soil," Dan Flannery said.

"What?"

"Soil," he repeated. "That's the word civilized people use. You need you a lesson or two in manners, young lady."

I folded up my hamburger wrapper and stood up to carry my milk glass to the sink. "Never mind," I said, turning to walk back to my room. "I think I figured out what dirt is."

"Soil!" Dan Flannery shouted after me.

In the night I woke up thirsty. I sat in bed, my heart heavy, dreading what came next. I reached over and cracked the venetian blinds to look outside, but the back-yard was all dark, like a black net waiting to cover you. I put my legs over the side of the bed and made them touch the floor.

Out in the kitchen it was there waiting. In the daylight

it was nothing, a clock, you forgot all about it, but at night each number shone, like a warning, a countdown. I had to touch each one, not hurrying. The blue glow almost made me sick. At the end I could fill a cup of water from the tap and swallow it down, my reward.

I stood there drinking when I heard a man's low laugh. It wasn't any other sound. It came from close by. I held the cup so tightly I thought it would crack. I didn't want to move. I watched the lighted point of the second hand sweep past the numbers. It took me almost a minute to understand. It was Dan Flannery laughing, down the hall, behind the closed door in Kit's bedroom.

You could just notice a thing that had been there all along, like gravity or electricity. Something everybody else knew. I thought of Sinclair looking down to skid the rock along the sidewalk. And Mrs. Swope making a face when the blue car turned into the driveway. I walked over to the kitchen window now and lifted the curtain. The car was out there, under the streetlamp, its metal grille like rows of teeth, laughing, too.

CHAPTER

11

In Beirut I had told lies to the other kids. On Saturdays
we took picnic lunches to the banyan tree or to the
wooded ledge above the university tennis courts. It would
be me, Jill Pillsworth, and two or three others, kids from
the embassy or the oil companies, who got dropped off
by their chauffeurs. They asked me about things like
hula hoops or color TV, things they'd only heard about
because even though they were supposed to be American,
they'd lived most of their lives in Beirut or other places,
Cairo, Riyadh, Rome.

At first I just told them the truth. I stood on a rock,
high above the tennis courts, waggling my hips to show
how you kept a hula hoop going. They were older than
I was, but they studied everything I did, memorizing.
They didn't know anything. So it was easy to start making
things up. I told them that you could ride ponies to school

in the States and that you could run Coca-Cola right out of a special tap in your sink. I said that at Christmas it always snowed and you could skate along the rivers from town to town. Only Jill Pillsworth doubted me. Her parents took her to visit her grandparents in Philadelphia almost every summer. She lifted her eyebrows, but she never stopped me. I said whatever I wanted to say. The other ones believed anything. I almost believed it, too. I could clearly see myself gliding down the frozen Cuyahoga River, I could feel the slash of the wind on my face. It didn't mean anything that I'd never ice-skated in my life.

One of the embassy kids, Hope, invited me over. Her maid brought out a tray of boughasha pastries for an after-school snack, and we ate at a big lacquered table, scattering filo crumbs onto the Turkish rug. The apartment was huge and modern with wide-open rooms. Smaller Turkish rugs were draped over the low sofas, and copper trays were hung on the walls, along with some painted masks. A hubble-bubble pipe was displayed on a shelf, where most people would put a china vase.

I looked at Hope, happily licking the walnut filling out of her cigar-shaped pastry as if it were a normal snack for school kids. Her face was wide and cheerful, the same as the rooms.

"How come those rugs are on the *furniture?*" I asked her. "Instead of on the floor?"

"I don't know," she said. "Do you want that last boughasha?"

I wanted an Oreo or even a Lorna Doone. I wanted to get away before it rubbed off, this affliction of forgetting how to be American. It was something you had to be vigilant about, or it would overtake you and you wouldn't even know. You'd be like Hope, smiling, hungry for boughasha.

"Go ahead," I told her pityingly, "you can have it."

Before long my mom started buying leather hassocks and then a camel saddle for our living room in Beirut. I complained to her that all the leather made my nose run.

"Get a hankie," she said, laughing.

She found a length of gold brocade at the open market and had it cut into an evening dress that curved around her shoulders. She and my dad went out to casinos and restaurants. They met a group of tourists from France and drove with them to Baalbek to watch the sun come up. Whenever I saw my mom getting ready to go out, I made up things: that my stomach hurt, that I had a sore throat, that my spelling homework was too hard. Bibi and Nell and Alize would all be there with me, but it wasn't enough. I wanted her. She would stay to do the things I wanted, to feel my forehead and fix me milk tea and drill me on spelling "whistle" and "mystery," but, I knew, afterward she would go. She would always go. You couldn't stop her. Her dress scared me. It was like golden wings.

Mrs. Pillsworth repeated to my mom several of the lies I had been telling. Of course, Jill had made them even bigger.

"You told the other girls that in the States people have tiny TVs that they carry around in their pockets? And that you can press a button in your bedroom and a Tootsie Roll comes out of a slot in the wall?"

"I just said *gum*," I protested. "Not a Tootsie Roll."

"Sweetie," Mom said, "imagination is good, but let's be clear on where truth begins and ends."

I looked down.

"Also," she said, "I don't know. All this glorifying of the United States. What disappoints me is that you're closing yourself off to other possibilities. The possibilities of the whole wide world!"

I shrugged, looking down. I already knew I was a disappointment.

At Bible School Mrs. Wilmott stood in front of us, smiling. "Girls," she said, "I've just made the most marvelous discovery!"

Sinclair leaned toward me. "She finally discovered Mr. Wilmott's thing."

"And it concerns Mia Veery."

"Uh-oh," Sinclair whispered. "*You* discovered his thing!"

"Ssh." I shoved her. Everybody was looking at me now. I blinked. Mrs. Wilmott's smile seemed full of meaning. They're coming home, I thought. It was what I always thought, what I'd think first forever.

But Mrs. Wilmott clasped her big, flat hands together and announced, "Girls, Mia can tell us all about what it's like in the Holy Land! I just learned that she's been living right there, near the area where all our Bible stories come from."

I felt all the eyes watching me. "You mean, Beirut?" I said finally.

"Come on, stand right up here, Mia, and talk to us about it." Mrs. Wilmott motioned me forward.

"About what?" I said, not moving.

"Beirut!"

"What about it?"

"Mia, dear, *we've* never been there. You can tell us anything!"

They were waiting. I slowly got to my feet. "The Mediterranean is very blue. And, um, they speak Arabic."

"And?" Mrs. Wilmott prompted. "It's so close to those places we've been reading about—Jerusalem, Nazareth, Galilee—isn't it?"

"Yeah." I had no idea. Geography was my weak subject. Cities and countries never settled themselves in my brain. At school in Beirut, when we were asked to stick a pin in the U.S. map to show where we were from, I stood for an agonizing time while my classmates looked on, my hand zigzagging all across the forty-eight states, searching for Ohio. When I began to hear laughter, I shoved the pin in and looked: Bad Axe, Michigan. I liked the sound of it. Later, when we had to give reports on our home states, I did a better job than anybody. I told about the truck farms above Muskegon where they grew apples and cherries. I knew about the automobile industry and the smelt fishing and the pockets of iron ore. The state bird was the robin. The state flower, the apple blossom. I had never been there, but with every detail it became my own. I even managed to learn its place on the map, up there at the top, mitten-shaped, surrounded by lakes. Michigan. It was mine.

With Beirut, though, it was the opposite. I only knew the real things, not the information from the *Hammond Atlas*. I would never say about my mom and the gold dress and Alize in the kitchen ironing shirts and singing. I didn't even want to say about the Saturday picnics on the ledge when the lizards came out to sun on the rocks and below, in the distance, we could watch the field of red poppies change shape every time the wind blew. The more I told, the more it seemed it would leak away, like a last glass of water. If it spilled, you could never have it back.

I sat down.

"Oh," Mrs. Wilmott said. "All right. Well, thank you, dear."

In the girls' rest room I stared in the mirror and touched my hair. There was nothing you could do with flat beige hair that just hung there. I was waiting for Sinclair. It was right after lunch, the time when everybody pushed into the rest room and lined up for the toilets. At the end of the row of sinks Lady-Anne leaned forward and bared her teeth, getting ready to brush them, before she clipped back into her headgear. It seemed so dutiful, like a horse that bent down to have the harness put on.

The door swung open, and it was Corinne and two of the others. They could make the room change by walking in together, by the way their eyes panned, like cameras. Today they wore stretch hairbands, pastel colors.

Lady-Anne bent forward to spit out foam in the sink.

That caught Corinne's eye. She stopped and spread her arms protectively in front of her friends. "Stay back, you-all," she said. "We don't know if Lady-Anne has had her rabies shot."

When they laughed, everybody laughed. It was their power, it was unexplainable. They walked on, and kids pressed back, making room for them.

Lady-Anne stuck her lip out. There was toothpaste on it. "I should tell on them." Her voice shook. "My mama said to tell if anybody makes fun of me because of my orthodontia."

I pulled a paper towel out of the dispenser. There were those kids who would never know. You shouldn't carry a tube of Pepsodent with you in your little straw bag. You shouldn't seriously say "orthodontia." I handed her the towel. "Here, you should wipe your mouth."

Sinclair and I walked downtown after Bible School. The stores were arranged in an orderly square around the city hall, a big brick building with white columns, not unlike Sinclair's own house.

"I think the Yankees took over that town hall or something," Sinclair said in a bored voice. Her mom had told her to show me the sights. We walked around to the side of the building to examine a cannon, a pyramid of cannonballs, welded together, and a scowling statue of General Braxton Bragg. The sun beat down. We stood, scuffing our feet in the gravel pathway under the general's disapproving stare.

"Yeah, so that's everything," Sinclair said after a minute. "Let's go get something to drink. I have money."

We drank orange Nehis at the counter at Woolworth's, and when we'd finished those, we ordered french fries. Sinclair paid. She had dollars wadded in the pocket of her shorts. The ceiling fans revolved above us. Woolworth's was as familiar as I'd known it would be. I ran my hand along the scarred Formica countertop. I picked up a sticky glass salt shaker and set it down.

"Guess what," Sinclair said.

"What?" Our french fries arrived on an oval plate. They were the thick, mealy kind I liked. I squeezed out a puddle of ketchup on the side.

Sinclair leaned toward me and said in a confidential tone, "I'm pretty sure I have inspiration."

"What's that?" I pushed a fry into my mouth.

"Inspiration! It's in the saints book. You know, the secret voice that tells you what you're supposed to do. Like slay a dragon or cut off all your hair or something."

"Oh," I said it calmly. "What did it tell you to do?" I wanted her to talk, not to guess from my face. Inspiration. So it had a name.

"Well, not exactly anything yet. This was just the first time. It was this morning. I was lying in bed, and it sang 'Sinclaaiirrr.'"

"It sang?"

"Yeah. Sinclaairrr," she trilled again.

That wasn't anything, maybe an oriole on a tree branch, but I didn't tell her that. I wouldn't ruin her hopeful face. Even if you didn't realize it at first, this must be part of how you picked your friends, guessing that they had something you wanted for yourself. Here she was, longing for a voice in the night to order her around. And more than anything just then I would have chosen to be the one who woke up each morning in the soft blue room just listening to a birdcall.

We looked at each other, and then we looked away, twisting on our stools. Sinclair poked at the empty oval plate, sliding it along the counter.

"Didn't those fries make you thirsty all over again?" she said finally.

I nodded.

"Let's get ice-cream sodas, but not here. At Bennie's they make the best."

Later we walked home, an indirect way, cutting down side streets to look at things: the house near the center of town that still had a wooden latrine in the yard; the foundation of the Holy Roller church that got struck by lightning and burned to the ground in one hour, killing four rattlesnakes that had been kept inside, caged up. You had to feel bad for them, burning up, trapped, even if they were rattlesnakes, Sinclair said, and I agreed. I told about the tarantulas with their graceful, furry legs in Beirut, how whenever they climbed the walls of the school building, kids smashed them, and they weren't hurting anybody, weren't even poisonous.

"I'd smash *them*!" Sinclair said. "Kids like that."

She led the way, in her slow, slouching walk, through the small streets. She knew where we were, but for me, one street wasn't distinguishable from another yet. The houses were low and even, like the ones on the Monopoly board. We turned a corner, and I stood still.

Dan Flannery's blue car was stopped there just ahead, its gloating metal grille unmistakable. The motor was idling, and Dan Flannery was there, visible through the windshield. There was a brown-haired woman next to him. They faced each other, not looking out, not noticing us.

"Mia?" Sinclair said. I was still standing in the middle of the sidewalk. I stepped over to the curb, crouching down behind a parked car and motioned to her.

"That's my aunt's boyfriend," I whispered when she'd squatted down next to me. "In that blue car."

"Yeah?" She popped her head up to see.

"Watch out! Are they looking?"

"Not at me," Sinclair said. "They're making goo-goo eyes."

I stood up then. I didn't care, I wanted him to see. The woman tipped her chin up, flirting; she had a long, skinny nose.

"She's uglier than your aunt," Sinclair whispered.

I reached down by the curb, grabbed a rock, and hurled it, hard. It hit the hood of the blue car with a loud crack and bounced off. Inside, they jolted apart as if they were electrocuted. Dan Flannery snapped his head around and noticed me then.

The car door flew open.

"Let's go." Sinclair was laughing, excited, pulling on my arm.

We ran back around the corner and down another similar street and then another, panting, checking over our shoulders for the blue car to come. Finally we slowed down, out of breath. I had a stitch in my side from running that hard after eating so much. I stopped to rub below my rib cage.

"Mia." Sinclair's eyes were shining. "You can say it. Something told you to throw that stone!"

I shook my head. "No," I said proudly, telling the truth. "I thought it up myself."

CHAPTER
12

The whole time my aunt was walking back and forth, slapping her hairbrush against her leg, I was thinking: Just hit me and get it over with. Dan Flannery had called to tell his side before I had a chance to come in the door.

"I don't understand you, I really don't. You could have injured somebody. He was meeting with a *client*. Somebody for *business*. What if they'd gotten hurt? What if you'd knocked anybody's eye out? Huh?" She slapped her own thigh with the white brush again. She must be making a good bruise there.

"I'll tell you. They'd take you away then, to someplace like the county *home*!" Slap. "And maybe, really, that would be for the best because God knows, I've done everything *I* know how to do. I'm done. I'm really *done*!" Slap-slap.

I squirmed in the chair she'd set me in. My stomach

wouldn't settle after that run through the streets. I was hot and sticky; my hair was like a wool cap pulled down over my ears. I just wanted my punishment, not all this.

"Blah, blah, blah," I said under my breath.

Kit stopped in her tracks. "Get out of my house," she said in a level voice.

I gaped at her.

"You heard me, get out!"

I slid low in my chair, looking up at her. "You can just spank me with that hairbrush. Go ahead."

"Oh, no." Kit tossed the white brush aside onto the sofa. "You don't dictate to *me* now. *Get up out of that chair.*"

I stood on the porch as she latched the screen behind me. She stepped back to close the heavy inside door that would really seal me out, like something final.

"You should be locking *him* out!" I screamed. "He was there necking! With some other *girlfriend.*"

The door clicked shut.

I rang the bell a few times, but nothing happened. I rattled the knob on the bolted back door. I ran around and around, nosing at the windows. The streets shimmered with the late-afternoon light. At the corner was the dried-up drainage ditch where you could find Indian money. Three houses down, a wide mimosa tree was spilling sweet pink feathers onto the grass. None of it tempted me now. I felt like those little dogs you see, pawing at the screen, only wanting in.

Finally, worn down, I sat on the front steps, just waiting. I couldn't tell how much time passed. I felt the stone step get cooler under my bottom. Men drove by, wearing gray uniform caps, returning from work at the cement plant. It was getting past the hour when Dan Flannery would have come with his hamburgers. My stomach was still full, but it was suppertime; somebody should feed me.

I crossed over to Mrs. Swope's house, and she met me at the door, as if she knew I was coming. Her fingers plucked at the top button on her housedress as she talked to me through the screen.

"I'm sorry for you, but, honey, I can't get between the two of you-all."

I stood a minute before I understood. She wouldn't take me in.

"Did she call you up?" I was starting to cry now. I had no place.

"Why, no," Mrs. Swope said. "I could hear the shouting. I don't know what it's all about, but it's between family, I don't want to take sides."

I sniffed back tears. I smelled sausage cooking inside. I saw back to the kitchen, where the light was on and the low blue flame flickered under the frying pan. "It's not just family, though," I cried. "It's because of Dan Flannery!"

She hesitated, fingering her button again. Her mouth worked, like chewing. "Go on," she said finally. "Honey, run on back. You know she'll let you in before long. You know she will."

I turned, rubbing both fists in my eyes.

"Aw, honey," she said, "maybe you've been acting too big for your britches."

Kit let me in by unlatching the door and saying, "All right." When I got up, stiffly, from the front steps, she had already walked off, leaving the door ajar. I went in, rubbing the kinks out of my legs, and saw she had set a place at the table and fixed an egg sandwich on a plate.

"That's for you," she said.

"Aren't you eating?"

"I'm not hungry."

I sat down at the table. She stayed standing, behind me, leaning against the drainboard. Nobody talked. I didn't want the sandwich then, but I felt her watching me as if her eyes could burn my back. I picked up the bread and bit.

"What made you think that was a *girlfriend?*" Kit said from behind me.

"What?" I put the sandwich down, wary. If I didn't say it right, everything would start up all over again.

"I mean, do you know what Dan's job involves? He sells the services of the printing company. He has to meet with all types of people in all kinds of places every single day!"

"Huh," I said. Out the window you could see the first lightning bugs of the evening, flashing as they rose out of the boxwood bushes.

"Of course, some of the people he meets with are

bound to be businesswomen," Kit said. "That's not surprising." She came over to the table and leaned down, rubbing at spots with a dishrag. Her hair hid her face. She swiped the wet rag, fiercely, around and around. "You can't just jump to conclusions because he drives by with a *business*woman in his car."

"Well, they weren't driving," I said. The kitchen was still except for the sliding sound of Kit's dishrag. I traced my fingers along the scalloped rim of my plate. "They were just parked outside a house."

"A house?" Kit's face turned toward me. "What street was this?"

"I don't know." What I remembered best was that the instant the rock cracked onto the blue car, I thought: Everything's changed now; you can't take it back.

"So I guess you got a good look at her," Kit said, wiping again. "I mean, if they were just stopped there, you could probably see everything."

"And she wasn't even pretty," I assured my aunt. "She had this big nose, and her hair was like Ahmar Beach."

"Ahmar Beach?"

"Near Beirut." I looked down, embarrassed. It was what I'd thought of, but out loud it hardly made sense, hair like a beach. "See, it doesn't have sand. It's all little brown periwinkle shells, in a pile."

"Periwinkle shells," Kit repeated. "God. Candy-Lee Echols?" She tossed down the dishrag. "Candy-Lee *Echols?* Let me think, she lives on—" She grabbed my shoulder. I felt the weight of her cast pressing down.

"Think now," she said, "where they were. It wasn't Luddy Street, was it?"

"I don't—"

"L-u-d-d-y, Luddy!" Kit said. "It runs right off French Street. Wait, I know!" She dashed across the room and pulled something out of the drawer by the telephone. "Here, look at this."

She spread out a street map of Ionia across the table, smoothing it flat, ignoring my plate underneath, with the uneaten egg sandwich.

"Okay," she said. "You were downtown first?"

"Yeah. Woolworth's. Then Bennie's."

"Okay, that would be about here."

She traced our route from the grid of roads around the town hall over to the Holy Roller church and then left onto French Street. I tried to pay attention, but it was a map. The crisscrossed colored lines were like when you took a radio apart. My eyes wouldn't focus.

"So then, off French, you took which one, do you think? The first right? The second?"

The streets were all the same, but I couldn't say that. She leaned close to me, and her skin was hot. Her casts had a smell, like feet. I squinted down at the map, trying, and after a while the lines snapped into place, matching with something real, the uneven sidewalks, the abandoned train tracks we'd crossed, the second right turn off French Street. All those blocks of look-alike houses were separate; you could find their names. It was like passing a test.

I pointed at the map and looked up, pleased, into my aunt's feverish face. "Luddy! It was Luddy."

I turned on both spigots, full force. I wished I had some of Kit's Calgon Bouquet to make the bathwater green and sweet, but I wouldn't dare to ask tonight. The way she was, she could put me back outside or really send me to the county home, even naked like this. I wrapped my arms around myself and climbed, shivering, into the hot bath.

There was a game I liked to play in the tub: how the world was made. I bent my knees to form mountains, rising from the floor of the sea. The rosy tips of my toes were chains of coral islands. The water, still rushing from the faucet, could be torrential rains or topical waterfalls, whatever I chose. I named new countries and invented whole populations to inhabit them. It could be different in any bath, depending on how deep I let the water get or if I decided to lie on my side, letting the wedge of my hip make one lone, curving continent. But always I was a kind ruler, making the rain stop in time, stirring the water just enough to cause the gentlest, warm waves to lap against the shore. And what I liked best, this was an orderly world. You knew where it began and ended, forever safe between the white porcelain walls.

When I turned the water off, Kit was talking in the kitchen. I couldn't make out the words, but from the aggrieved pitch of her voice I worried that she was complaining about me. I jumped up and padded, dripping, across the bath mat to open the door a crack. My aunt stood at the end of the short hallway, just inside the kitchen. The black telephone receiver was tucked in below her ear.

"No!" she said bitterly. Her shoulders hunched up. "You tell me. Is it better with her? Two arms that work, is that it?" She raised one hand, with her fingers spread, touching her own face. "I guess you find her more attractive," she said. "How she does herself up. I guess that's what you like." She dropped her fingers down. "Well, maybe I should have put little curls all over my head!" She gave a short, awful laugh. "Is that where I went wrong?"

I got back in the bath, but that fast, while I was out, the water had cooled. I had to run in more hot so I could fix up my world how I needed it to be, calm and warm, just safe again.

CHAPTER

13

Mrs. Wilmott tweeted on her pitch pipe, and we hummed back. She bent her head down. "No. No. No," she said. "You're still not getting it! Once more."

"Hmmmm." This time was worse. We sounded like the dial tone.

"All right." She seemed close to tears. "At least we put in our best effort, though, didn't we! Girls, we are true Commandments!"

We looked down. Nobody laughed out loud. She still thought we were nice, that we tried. You couldn't hate her.

It was lunchtime, so we settled in at our usual places, opening our bags and squinting into the heat that reflected off the parking lot and made the outlines of the buildings blur. It seemed to me that the routine of Bible School was something you could parse, like a sentence. Hymns, homily, projects, color guard: All the parts were just there to wrap around lunch, our free time, the heart of the sentence.

Sinclair poked me with her sharp elbow.

"Ow." I rubbed my arm.

"That's him," she said, nodding. "Yonder with the basketball."

I looked. He wasn't special, just a tall boy with a long, almost rubbery face and light hair cut high, leaving pink rims over his ears. He threw the ball and ran, his arms dangling.

"It's Eugene Foss," Sinclair said. "He's always looking at you. See, he just now looked!"

"Ssh!" I ducked my head, blushing. "Maybe he's looking at *you*."

"Uh-uh," Sinclair said. "I've known him since the second grade. I can tell which way he's looking."

I used my napkin to blot my damp, flushed neck. In Beirut it was hot, but I had never known anything like the Tennessee air. It had a thickness, like something jellied. Your skin was always slick. In the afternoons the sparrows walked sideways along the telephone wires as if they didn't have the will to fly.

"Whew," I said, sniffing, "I smell horses."

Sinclair gave me an odd smile.

"Don't you smell it?"

"It's me," she whispered. She looked all around, making certain nobody else was listening. "It's my hair shirt."

I sat back from her, wrinkling my nose. "Well, you should wear a different shirt, Sinclair. That one smells."

"No, you don't get it." She turned to me, her face bright. "I made it on purpose. I took the horse hairs out of the grooming comb and glued them into my undershirt. A *hair* shirt. You wear it to suffer, like the saints did. See, I'm going to wear it every day."

I smoothed my empty lunch sack in my lap, over and over, as if I could push the soft wrinkles out of the paper. A hair shirt. With horse hairs.

"Sinclair, that's going to get really itchy," I said finally.

"Yeah." Sinclair squirmed happily. "It already is."

We weren't alike. I touched the neck of my cotton jersey for reassurance. I would never be that way, choosing something smelly and repulsive, something not normal. I looked at Sinclair's strange, springy hair, her glowing eyes. I watched her lift one arm to scratch, with gusto, deep in the armpit. Unaccountably, how I felt was jealous.

For more than a week now Dan Flannery hadn't come over. Kit didn't say his name. She had started to work on maps sent over by the printing company. When I came in from Bible School, she was usually at the kitchen table, bent down, frowning at her proofs. When she looked up, her mouth stayed that way, pulled into a frown. She wore her bathrobe most of the day, sometimes getting dressed just before Hatty, the secretary from work, came by to pick up or deliver more proofs.

Hatty was tall and big-boned with a flat white face and a surprising slash of crimson lipstick. You could call her homely or exotic; I couldn't make up my mind. She always sat for a while, drinking iced tea with bourbon and telling Kit the stories from the office, and she brought me paper doll sets that they produced at the printing plant. They were of movie stars, and I got the ones that didn't turn out. Ink-blemished Sandra Dees. Kim Novaks with wide, brave smiles even though they were missing the tops of their heads. I was too old for paper dolls, but I liked fixing up these maimed ones. I patched them with tape and corrected their misshapen features with colored pencil. I designed tinfoil turbans to complete the Kim Novaks. It was satisfying, figuring out the best way to get them pretty again.

The nights were harder than ever now. We each fixed our own sandwiches and ate them when we wanted to. Kit usually carried hers off to her room or to the sofa in the front room, where she folded the newspaper open to the crossword puzzle and frowned down at it. If she put on the hi-fi, it was always to play jazz records with the horns that sounded like crying. I retreated to my own room to work on the paper dolls or read one of the old books stored there that had belonged to my mom and my aunt when they were young. They all seemed to be books about unlikely goody-goody children, like Honey Bunch or the Five Little Peppers. But I read them anyhow, mostly to touch the same pages that my mom might once have touched, too.

In the middle of the dark nights I would wake up

knowing. They were never coming back. It was the same as knowing the night would never end. I propelled myself out of bed and ran into the kitchen where the clock face waited. Touching the numbers was routine now, too simple. I had to do more, always more.

I had to open the door that led to the attic stairs and stand at the bottom, slowly counting to one hundred, while the smell of old, forgotten things floated down, like a blanket that could cover you. I had to reach under the sink and take out the cleanser bottle with the leering, bald genie on the label and kiss his malicious face three times. And finally, I had to take the flashlight out of the drawer, press it behind my fingers, and switch it on to confront the unthinkable outline of bones, my own skeleton made visible.

When morning came back and the light showed in the window, it was because I'd been good, doing everything I had to do. Sometimes, as a reward, I allowed myself to telephone Mr. Burton's office, the same as before. If somebody from an office in Washington was out looking, it must mean there was still a reason to look. Just to hear the voice answer, "Middle East," each time was as good as a promise.

"Well, she's strutting all around the accounting department looking like the cat who swallowed the canary," Hatty said.

"What a tramp," Kit said, shaking the melting ice cubes in her glass. "And you can quote me."

They were sitting on the porch. My aunt was in the swing with map layouts spread around her. I stood just inside the dim front hallway, out of sight.

"Oh, boy, you know she's terrified of when *you* come back to work!" Hatty said. "She must have asked me twenty times how much longer you'd be out."

"I ought to pop in for a surprise visit. Just to give her a heart attack!"

"Wouldn't that serve her right!"

It was quiet then, except for the squeak of the porch swing. I willed them to go on, to say more. I didn't want Hatty to drain her glass and stand up to leave. She always had someplace to go. She played duplicate bridge and was on a bowling team. Other evenings she took lessons in things: square dancing and rug hooking. She had an apartment in a new complex across town and two Manx cats, Stubble and Mister. I dreaded the moment each afternoon when she would take off to attend to some piece of her full, cluttered life, leaving Kit and me there to face our own vast and empty evening.

"I don't know, though." Kit shook her glass again. Beads of water dripped onto the maps below. "I wouldn't want to come in if it means running into *him* right now."

"I know." Hatty twisted her red mouth. "Why give yourself that aggravation?"

"Let's be realistic while we're at it." Kit held up her bandaged fists. "I can't drive. I can hardly hold a pencil.

Every line on every map takes me five times as long as it should. I won't be back for a while. Quite a while."

"Well, you deserved you a little rest, think of it like that."

"Ho, some *rest!*"

"Yeah, well, kids are a lot of work, I guess."

"Some more than others," Kit said. "Take my word for it."

"Aww, well, keep your chin up, sugar." Hatty picked up her empty glass and stood up. "Hey, I'm going to have to scoot."

I pushed open the screen door and went out, my feet slapping sulkily on the concrete.

"Well, here she is!" Hatty said. "Hi and good-bye."

"Wait," I said. "I thought you would come look at the paper dolls." My voice was whiny in my own ears. "I want you to see how I fixed Connie Stevens. In my room."

"Mia," Kit said sternly, "Hatty has someplace else to go."

I scowled in my aunt's direction.

"Isometric exercise!" Hatty said. "That's tonight!"

"And you can wipe that rude expression off your face," my aunt said to me. "This instant."

I looked at Hatty, standing, clutching her purse. She wanted to go, but she wanted us happy first. "As you two can probably tell," she said, "I need my exercise to get rid of *this*." She turned and slapped her round bottom.

We were silent.

"Because I have what's known as a Crisco shape!" Hatty smiled back and forth, between us, as if she could weave us together that way. "Fat in the can!"

"Eugene." I whispered it into the mirror. My heart didn't thud. Why couldn't he have a good name, Brad or Lance? I hugged myself, sliding my hands lovingly up and down my sides, to see how a boy's touch would feel. Instead I felt my own ribs under my fingertips. It was like rubbing your hands along a spiral notebook binder.

I turned out the light, sighing, and crossed the room to my bed. It wasn't completely dark out yet. The sky was no color you could name. I could stay up, but I didn't see the point. I was ready to let the day go.

Mrs. Swope paid me to help with chores. I tied strings around stacks of old newspapers and carried them out to her shed. I scraped yellowed wax from the edges of the floor with a kitchen knife and swept it into the dustbin.

"All right now," Mrs. Swope said. "Our next project is to eat up this carton of ice cream so I can defrost the freezer."

We sat at the table with the contents of the refrigerator spread all around us: small jars of Miracle Whip and sweet pickles, a quart of buttermilk, things for one person.

"We used to go pearling," Mrs. Swope told me. "Did you ever hear of that, pearling?"

I shook my head. The ice cream numbed my tongue. It was French vanilla, heavy, golden-colored.

"Well," Mrs. Swope said, "it isn't just oysters that give out pearls, the way most people think. In the old days we used to get them from mussels that we took out of the streams right here, in this part of Tennessee. Sometimes we'd find them in Lime Creek that runs back yonder, by the grammar school, but the big thing was to go out toward Cummingsville to the Caney Fork."

The icebox door was propped open. A pan on a shelf caught the melting water. I sat, twirling my spoon, waiting. Every time the water dripped into the pan, I could let myself have another bite of ice cream. But not until the drip. I waited.

"Your sweetheart was supposed to fetch you a pearl," Mrs. Swope continued. "We girls stayed on the riverbank and watched. Too dainty to stick our feet in the mud!" She removed her glasses and cleaned them with a paper napkin. "I had me quite a collection. A string with six pink Caney Fork pearls."

"From Mr. Swope?"

"Oh, honey, no. Other boys. Just boys, a long time ago." She rubbed her eyelids. "By the time I met Wish Swope, he was home from the Great War and I was twenty-eight years old, almost a spinster! We were married within a year. That's how it was then. You didn't need to think twice. You found a good man and you decided to love him. And you just stayed true."

It was just how I thought things ought to be. You followed the rules, and you got to live a regular life. I would never understand why people wanted anything else.

"But then, in those years after the war, that's when

the pearls got scarcer and scarcer until you couldn't find a one." She hooked her glasses back on. Her ears seemed shaped from something soft, like what they use for moccasins. "It was because they were building all those dams then. The rivers shifted so even the little creeks changed course. Then they weren't the same, for the mussels to grow there."

"That's terrible!" Wiping out pearls and the olden days and staying true to your sweetheart. It wasn't right that what you needed most could be swept away, just like that. "If I had dynamite, I'd blow up those dams!"

"I know, honey," Mrs. Swope said. "But the dams do us good, too. They're making us our electric, don't you see? To run the lights and the toaster and the TV. The hot water. The Frigidaire. Why, think where we'd be without them!"

But I didn't want to think. There were just choices you should never have to make. Love or electricity. Pearls or the TV. America or your mom and dad. I stirred my soupy ice cream, waiting. This was the best, no choosing, only doing what you had to do. Spoon poised, I listened, ready for the next drip.

Our last project of the morning was to dust shelves in the living room. Mrs. Swope explained who was who in all the pictures in the picture frames. Her only child, a son, was called Buddy, or at least he used to be. Now he was an important engineer in Georgia, and he went by the name Wishart Swope, Jr. His wife was Kay, and they had two daughters, close to my age, with fancy names,

Juliette and Michelle. They took voice coaching and private baton. In the pictures they had dark eye makeup and tiaras, askew on their curly heads. Across their chests were sashes with the titles they'd won: Little Miss Peachtree and Southern States Peanut.

"They won more, too, but I forget them all," Mrs. Swope said. "All that foolishness." She held up each picture and brushed it with her fingers as if she could stroke their faces. "It keeps them too busy to visit their old grandmaw!"

"Well, I don't have a real grandmother." I stared down, shyly, at the old dish towel I was using to dust. "But if I could get one, like a pretend one, I sure would visit her. Every day."

"Bless your heart, honey, I bet you would!" Mrs. Swope tousled my mousy hair. "I don't guess you'd be one for the beauty pageants anyhow."

In Sinclair's bedroom we took the four white pillows off the beds and scattered them on the blue rug, like clouds in the sky. It was supposed to be heaven. We were saints looking down, dealing with sinners.

"I see Mr. Wilmott!" Sinclair peered through her curled fingers, like binoculars. "Hmm. He's out behind the church shed, kissing Jeannie."

"Jeannie!" I was shocked.

"Well, yeah." Sinclair looked at me. "Don't be such a prude. It couldn't be a sin if we just had him kissing his wife." She raised her binoculars again. "So their lips are together, Mr. Wilmott and Jeannie."

"I don't know," I said. "It just makes me feel bad for Mrs. Wilmott."

"Their mouths are open." Sinclair continued, ignoring me. "And their tongues touch."

I forgot Mrs. Wilmott then. I waited for more.

"He starts to unbutton her blouse." Sinclair said. "The top button. The second button."

My own chest was on fire.

"The third button. His fingers reach in—"

"Yeah?" I breathed.

"*Zap!* A lightning bolt shoots down and kills them!"

"What!" I sat up on my pillow. "That wasn't a good ending."

Sinclair shrugged. "That's how *you* wanted to play. You said the sinners should get punished in the end."

"Well, not like that," I said crossly. "Not so suddenly, in the middle of the story."

Sinclair's parents took us to the country club for dinner. Her mom drove while her dad sat, rubbing his temples and smoking cigarette after cigarette.

"That's what he's always like on Fridays," Sinclair explained in the backseat. "Migraines. From a whole week of the glue fumes at work."

He was an extremely tall man with the same sloping posture as Sinclair's. He owned a company that made shoe boxes, but his interest was in music. Before we got in the car, he had sat on the piano bench with his eyes closed and a cigarette between his lips. He arched his nicotine-stained fingers and held them just above the keyboard as if it were enough, just the idea of the song.

"You'll hate it at the country club," Sinclair assured me. "It has the most snobby, boring people in the world. But the food is good." She scratched her chest, adding a strong horse odor to the dense, smoky air. "That's the only reason we go, to not starve. Which we would at home since *everybody's* too lazy to cook on the weekends."

"Busy, darling," her mom said. "Not lazy."

The club's dining room was lit by four enormous, sparkling chandeliers, and what you heard when you walked in was not talking but the scrape of the heavy silverware against the china plates. To get the food, you walked up to a long table loaded with steaming metal dishes and platters with big slabs of dripping meat.

Black men wearing white coats stood behind the table, waiting to do what you asked them to do, ladle the soup or carve the beef. They awed me; they seemed like something famous.

"Are those slaves?" I whispered to Sinclair.

"Right! Exactly!" She socked my arm, laughing, bewildering me. "So now you see what I meant about this place!"

I followed her down the line, from dish to dish, only daring to choose what she chose. At the end of the table she held out her plate to a man wearing a white chef's hat.

"Hey, George."

"And hey yourself, Miss Smith," he answered back. He smiled, and I knew instantly where I had seen him before. He really was somebody famous.

"Rare, please, George," Sinclair said.

I stepped up next and held out my plate. "Rare, please, George," I repeated. He handed back the plate with the pink slices. "Thank you," I said. I glanced up into his dark, kind face, the unmistakable tall hat. "At first I didn't recognize you," I told him shyly, "because I haven't seen a Cream of Wheat box in three years. They don't sell it in Beirut, where I was, but I still remember it and your picture on it."

He stood still, holding the giant fork and knife over the top of the meat.

"But I'll get some, now that I'm back," I promised. "I always liked Cream of Wheat!"

He stared down at the tablecloth. "Yes'm," he said finally.

"Nice to meet you," I told him. I turned to join Sinclair at the table full of pies.

After we ate, Sinclair and I went outside. It was all kids out there, running on the edge of the golf course in the twilight while the parents stayed inside in the air conditioning. Sinclair and I crossed the lawn and kept going, as if we had a destination, over the low ridges of the golf course, past flags and pits of sand, the sweep of grass and the broad, dusky sky just pulling us farther and farther out. We stopped when we got to a small pond, shaped like an uneven heart.

"Hey, try this," Sinclair said. She pulled off her shoes and sat down, sticking her feet down into the dark water.

I did it, too, and she watched me, smiling, expecting something.

"Agh!" My feet flew out of the water, and I jumped up.

"Minnows!" Sinclair lolled back in the grass, laughing. "It's only itty-bitty minnows."

I saw them then, a thousand darting silver shapes below the surface of the water. "It felt like they were biting me."

"They kind of were," Sinclair said, "but really, it's okay when you get used to it."

I sat back down next to her, hugging my knees, keeping my feet up, out of the water. The crickets were starting, far off in the privet hedges. There were no lights out here, just a tiny slice of moon like a fingernail paring.

"We could be anywhere," I said. "We could be some-place in the wilderness."

"I guess," Sinclair said. "But to me it's just the water trap on the thirteenth hole where my brothers used to force me to jump in and pick up all the golf balls on the bottom."

"Where are your brothers anyhow?"

"One's in Europe, and one's at tennis camp."

I hugged my knees tighter. My sisters had given up writing to me since I never wrote back. If anybody asked, I couldn't say where they were or when I'd even see them again.

Stars had popped out overhead, but they were still faint, as if the sky weren't quite ready for its show. Once my mom had taken me across the Corniche and down onto the slippery rocks below to point out Vega, an important star for navigators. It hung low over the horizon, greenish gold, like a variety of apple, all alone on a bottom branch.

"Let's just sit and watch it for a while," my mom said.

"These rocks are too slimy," I complained. "I want to go back inside."

"Oh, come on." She sat herself down cross-legged, head thrust forward, staring. I stood stiffly behind her and glared at the sky.

"It's ravishing, you know," she said after a while. "I think it's the most beautiful thing I've ever seen."

I reached down and covered her eyes with my two hands.

Sinclair sighed now, leaning back on her elbows, looking up at the hazy stars. "I keep on waiting for more messages," she said. "Inspiration. I don't know. Maybe I might try sleeping on a hard wooden plank or something."

I lowered my feet cautiously back into the warm black pond, watching the minnows swarm. Music started in the distance, fervid chords on a piano.

"Oh, no." Sinclair stood up. "We have to go. That's the guy at the club who thinks he's Liberace. We always go home when he starts playing. It's pure agony to my dad."

"Okay, just a minute." I lingered, paralyzed by the wonderful torture of the silver minnows. They charged at my legs as if they loved me or needed me, as if they could pick me clean with just their kisses.

CHAPTER
15

I snooped in my aunt's bedroom while she took a bath.
I opened drawers and stuck my hands between the light
layers of nylon slips and underwear. I twisted the caps
off lotions and poked a finger in to get their smell. I
wanted something, but I didn't know what.

The walls were a deep rose color; the floor was wood
that had lost its shine. You couldn't call the room messy
exactly, but there were dresses tossed over the back of
the rocking chair and opened books, lying facedown, on
the floor around the unmade bed. When I first came to
Kit's house, she had everything arranged and orderly in
a way I had never seen in a house. The books were
matched by height and color on the shelves. There were
small bars of wrapped soaps by the bathroom sink, like
a hotel. Even in the days after she came home with her
broken arms, she kept her standards up. I remembered

the surprise of opening her closet while I was helping her get dressed and finding the shoes, all black and white pumps, aligned precisely on the wooden rack, like a little choir standing up, ready to sing.

Now in the closet shoes were lying where they'd been kicked off, and along with the pumps there were sandals and rubber thongs and a pair of matted blue plush slippers that had all appeared from somewhere. It was like a riddle you couldn't solve. The more clues she left lying around, the more mysterious she seemed.

I climbed into her bed and fitted my head into the crater her head had shaped in the soft white pillow. I leaned down and picked up one of the opened books from the floor. *Collected Poems* by Edna St. Vincent Millay. I studied the page Kit had been reading. It was what I expected, poetry, full of unyielding words such as *hepaticas* and *mullein*, but I read the lines over and over, determined to make the meaning come clear, the same way the road map had suddenly shifted into focus that day, at the kitchen table.

Parts of it weren't difficult. The woodpecker tapping in the orchard, the still, deep streams, the sunny hillside. Those things made sense. They were things I already knew. But as I read them again and again, I saw that those easy images weren't the best. There were other, more unlikely pairings of words that you had to stop and pick apart like a complicated knot. And when you did it, your heart beat because they were so true. It seemed as if there couldn't be anything truer. "Of dazzling mud," it said in the poem, and every time I read it, my breath caught there. Dazzling mud!

"What the—what are you *doing?*"

My aunt stood in the doorway, a pink towel wrapped around her, the ends of her hair in wet points against her neck.

"Reading." I held up the book to show her.

"Oh, *reading.*" She pinched the towel across her freckled chest. "I see. And that sure explains what you're doing with *my* book, lying in *my* bed."

I didn't have an answer. I sat up. She was like a flamingo, draped in pink with the long neck above, the long legs below. You could make that into a poem somehow, including her dingy bands of plaster where there should be wings.

"This is really the last straw," Kit said. She strode into the room, kicking a book across the floor. "I'm not prepared to give up every vestige of my privacy. Really, I think I've given up enough, Mia."

She paced toward the wall, then pivoted back in my direction. Her face was pulled into its new frown. "Do I lie around in *your* bed? Do I?"

I shook my head, but she wasn't looking at me.

She paced and turned again. "Well, it's time some people started thinking about *me!*" She thumped her chest bone with her fist. "You don't need to come in here again until I invite you. It's my room. It's *my* life!" She thumped her cast up against her chest again, and suddenly I recognized the gesture. It tied in with everything, the littered room, the poetry books, all the frowning.

"Ha," I said. "I get it!"

"I hope you do," Kit said.

"High drama!" I thumped my own chest happily, pleased with the hollow sound it made, pleased with myself for figuring it all out. "Like you showed me that day. You're trying to act how a teenager would act!"

Kit stood rock still, gripping her towel. "What?" she said. "I'm—" She shook her head. "No, I'm—" She stopped again and then fixed her gray eyes on me. "You are *still* in my bed!" she yelled.

"I'm going, I'm going." I slid off the crumpled sheets. "Could I please borrow this book?"

"Give me that," Kit said.

I sighed and handed her the book.

"Now go."

I went.

I understood the frenzied look on all those saints in the pictures now. Inspiration or whatever it was wouldn't let you rest. It pushed harder and harder once it had you listening. It made me turn around the needlepoint pillow on the sofa, hiding the picture my grandmother had painstakingly stitched, an owl with beaded yellow eyes. Kit, frowning, leaned down and restored it to its owl side every so often, but each time, as soon as she left the room, I flipped it back, the way it had to be. I couldn't give a reason for this or for any of the other new things I had to follow: no drinking milk on Monday, Wednesday, or Friday; no eating bananas, ever; and first thing every morning, I was obliged to choose a single hair to pluck from my head and toss out the back door so it could be lifted by the breeze and carried off anywhere in the world. No reasons were necessary; you couldn't even ask. Sometimes I turned quickly to the mirror when I passed by, afraid I might catch a glittering saint face looking back, but always, luckily, it was still just me.

Hatty was going to fix us dinner. She carried in a grocery sack and set it down, heavily, on the counter. I was in a kitchen chair, swinging my legs, waiting for her.

"Boo," I said.

She spun around, a hand at her throat. "Whew, child, you took ten years off my life!" She reached into her sack and pulled out a cardboard sheet of paper dolls. "Here you go."

It was Annette Funicello with too much yellow in her skin tone, the same one she'd brought the last time. "Thank you," I said politely.

"Aw, I know," Hatty said. "You're thinking, Who needs another Annette with jaundice!"

"No, that's okay. It's just hard to fix her right. I colored on that last one, and she came out orange."

"Huh." Hatty shrugged. "Well, it was slim pickings in

the seconds pile today. She was what I could get. Of course," she added in a confidential voice, "everybody was in there hunting after poor old Marilyn Monroe."

"How come?"

Hatty's red mouth opened in surprise. "You haven't heard? She's dead! They found her like that in bed this morning. And she was the same age as me! Don't you-all listen to the news in this house?"

"We don't have a TV that works."

"Oh, I know." Hatty shook her head. She reached down into her sack and began unloading cans onto the counter. "But it goes deeper than that. Sometimes you two, I don't know. It's just the way you are, you could be from Mars!"

I touched my face worriedly. Maybe it did show there, somehow, everything I wanted to hide.

The counter was lined with cans and jars. Hawaiian pineapple. Water chestnuts. Maraschino cherries. "You-all are in for a treat," Hatty assured me. "Polynesian chop suey."

"Now, *that* sounds cosmopolitan!" My aunt swept into the kitchen and greeted Hatty with a kiss on the cheek. Kit was wearing a sleeveless dress and several long strands of clattering wooden beads. Her hair was twisted up on her head and secured with a rectangle of leather that had something like a skewer stuck through it.

Hatty and I stood and stared.

"I, for one, am ready for a culinary change of pace," Kit said. "I am just so weary of the same old same-old." She noticed us staring then. "Well, what?" she said irritably. "Can't a person do anything new around here? Is it against the *law*?"

At dinner she insisted on singing us a song she'd learned from the radio. We put down our forks and sat with our hands in our laps to listen. My aunt sang in a high, shaking voice about how the answers are blowing in the wind. Each time you put your hands up to clap, it turned out that the song wasn't over. I looked up at the light that flickered on the white ceiling from the candles Hatty had set up and then back down, across the table at my aunt, flushed and intent, starting another verse.

Later Hatty fixed us all fancy drinks to carry into the living room. She and Kit talked about Marilyn Monroe and somebody from the printing plant who almost lost a thumb when a spring bolt on a machine misfired. My drink was Nehi, dressed up with a row of cherries and a sliver of orange, speared on a toothpick. I sipped it slowly, afraid that when it was gone, they would send me to bed.

"Well, it might be that I won't come back at all," Kit told Hatty. "Who knows?"

"Now, don't let *him* drive you right out of a good job."

"Oh, I don't give a hoot what he thinks! It's not that."

"But, honey, you've worked there fourteen years."

"That's just what I'm saying," Kit said.

When the drinks were all gone, Hatty winked at me and took up the glasses to fix another round. We set up the card table to play a game of Scrabble. The clock on the mantelpiece chimed, and I sat still in my chair, waiting for my aunt to look up and say, "Oh, bedtime," but she didn't.

I wrote down the scores for Scrabble. It was almost too easy, playing against them. They didn't use strategy, the way I'd learned from my dad and my sisters. You had to remember the two-letter words from the dictionary like *op* and *pi* and also the unusual and highly valuable words like *zax* and *zarf.*

"Mia, you're beating the pants off us old ladies," Hatty said. She put down *lid.* Four points. I smiled down, filling it in on the scorepad.

"She's smart," Kit said quietly.

I looked up then, but she stared at her letters, eyes narrowed in concentration. Finally she plucked several tiles off the rack and set them down on the board, positioning them with one finger: *t y r o.*

"What the heck is that?" Hatty said.

"It's my word," Kit said, "obviously."

"Well, pardon *me*," Hatty said, "if I don't happen to recognize every obscure word in the English language."

"It's hardly obscure," Kit said. "If—"

"Wait, are you challenging her?" I asked Hatty. "Because if you're challenging her, in the rules you have to—"

"Oh, for crying out loud!" Kit sat back from the table, scowling at both of us. "Tyro!" she cried. Her hair was sliding out of its clasp. "Somebody with very little experience! Who still makes mistakes. Somebody who's only just figuring things out!"

"Write that down," Hatty advised me.

Tyro. A waste of a *Y.* Seven points after all that fuss. I wrote it down.

When they finally did send me to bed, so late, there was something hard on the pillow. I picked it up and put on the light, and I was holding the book of poems.

CHAPTER

16

It had been raining. I remembered it drumming on the window in the night, but now there were just high dull clouds, the color of pewter. I was walking to Bible School along the darkened pavement, and on the lawns around me there were webs stretched like doilies over the grass, glistening with raindrops. In Ohio our teacher used to tell us this was from fairies doing their laundry. Miss Hoffmeyer. That was first grade, when they still talked about fairies. Everything was possible then. Miss Hoffmeyer speaking to us in her flat Ohio voice that you didn't doubt: "Look outside, boys and girls, it's the fairies' washday again." Warsh-day, she said it.

"Mia!" Sinclair called to me from the end of the block. I waited for her to catch up. She was walking even more slowly than usual. Her hair spiraled out on all sides in the damp air. "Here," she said when she caught up to

me, "I brought you something." She held out a flattened
Milky Way bar. "I sat on it, though."

"Thanks." I dropped it into my lunch sack.

"That's not even the bad one," Sinclair assured me. "I
sat on mine worse."

We passed the tailor shop that had orange cellophane
over the windows for keeping out the sun, and then
we turned, following the church driveway around to the
parking lot. Sinclair lagged behind. I could see now she
was actually limping, placing one foot tenderly in front
of the other.

"What are you doing?" I said. "Did you hurt your
feet?"

She shook her head mysteriously.

"Sinclair," I said, "come *on*. What is it?"

"Oh, I just put gravel in my shoes," she said. "To see
if I could make myself walk on it." She had that odd,
faraway smile again, pleased with herself.

"Well, you walked on it," I said. "You can dump it
out now."

"Nah, I'm not ready yet."

"So, what are you going to do? Go around like a
crippled person all day?"

"Maybe. If I want to."

"Sinclair, that's not even how inspiration works! You
don't even know. You don't *choose* weird things to do. It
just—"

I stopped myself. Sinclair watched me, her inky eyes
shining. "Go on," she said.

"Oh, never mind!" I said. "Go ahead and be crippled. Limp all over the place! But I'm not waiting around for you." I strode off, swinging my arms extravagantly, stepping down hard in my painless, ordinary shoes.

Mrs. Wilmott read us the lesson of the day. She sat precariously on a small piano stool in front of us, her plaid skirt tucked around her long legs. The confusing names and events in the Bible made my mind wander. Jehovah. Jabash. Gilead. Streams of flowing honey. I liked the sound of it all, but it didn't make sense as a story.

"In time Jacob became very *wealthy*." Mrs. Wilmott read earnestly, making her voice rise and dip. "He had large flocks, slaves, and *many* asses."

Some girls snickered. Lady-Anne turned around to glare at all of us.

"What?" Mrs. Wilmott peered over the top of the book, smiling, ready to share the joke. Her long feet twisted around the tripod of the piano stool. One push and over she would go, straight down, like felling a tree.

If you looked around, you saw the rows of little girls wearing plastic barrettes and Lady-Anne trussed up in metal wires and Sinclair, off to one side, dreamily, continuously scratching her chest. I shifted around, irritably, on the tarpaulin that had been spread on the wet grass for us to sit. I only wanted to be somewhere else. I wanted somebody to say, "Oh, there's been a mistake; you should be in with the normal ones." When it was time for lunch,

I bolted up and away from them all so fast my head went light.

In the girls' room a cluster of Devotions stood, blocking the sinks. They were drawing with colored pens on one anothers' arms, forming tattoos of daisies and hearts and stars.

I said, "Excuse me," in a loud voice and pushed sideways with my hip to get through. They stopped talking and looked at me as I stepped up to the sink. I felt reckless, almost giddy. "I can draw good butterflies," I announced. "Here, I'll show you."

I took pens right out of the hand of the startled girl next to me and bent down to work on my own arm. I didn't think about it. I just drew an orange and black painted lady, intricate with dots and shadings and filigreed edges. When I finished, it was upside down, but it didn't matter. I had the best tattoo.

"Aren't you the one that climbed the water tower that time and had the write-up in the paper?" asked the girl whose pens I'd borrowed.

I nodded modestly. "Ummhmm. And I got a concussion." The room was silent; all the attention was on me.

"Make me one of those butterflies," a voice commanded. "Only right side up." It was Corinne Hilt, extending her arm.

As I traced the black pen over her skin, all the bravado I'd felt a few minutes earlier drained away. How had I done it? Who did I think I was, standing here among the Devotions, holding on to the long, golden arm of their leader? My hand shook, but I worked on, filling in the tiny detail, making her butterfly more brilliant and delicate than my own. When it was done, she looked back and forth from my arm to hers, pursing her mouth, satisfied.

"Why don't you come eat lunch with us," she said, not asking.

I picked up my sack, and we went off, simple as that, secure in a bunch, all tattooed.

At lunch they were nice, sharing potato chips and Moon Pies. They asked me where I lived before, and I said Ohio, skipping everything that would need to be explained. I was happy then, just sounding like a regular kid. I told them that I could dance the twist and that my boyfriend, Brad, wrote me letters every week from Ohio and that I had two older sisters who were away, at tennis camp.

They showed me how to turn a handspring, vaulting over and over through the film of damp air, with my eyes shut. I breathed in so hard I got the hiccups, and then they grouped around me, thumping my back and arguing over the best cures: tickling my feet, drinking water upside down, putting ice down my shirt.

I sat very still, between the racking hiccups, just wanting it to go on and on, the lilt of their voices talking about me, the reassuring weight of so many hands clapping my back.

"Mia?"

I looked up. Sinclair was standing a few feet away, on the pavement, twisting her lunch sack nervously. "Uh," she said. " 'O beautiful for spacious skies.' "

I stared at her.

"Hey, Sinclair," Corinne said, "why don't you trot on back to your stable?"

"Mia," Sinclair repeated, ignoring Corinne. " 'O beautiful for spacious *skies*.' The code!"

I hiccuped drunkenly.

"Sinclair, nobody even knows what you're talking about, so just beat it." Corinne flicked her hand, like shooing a bug.

"Mia knows," Sinclair said stubbornly. "She knows."

They looked at me. I could feel the hands drop away from my back.

"Sure, I know," I said. "It's a song. But why's she singing it at *me*?"

Sinclair stood there for a second, her twisted, saggy lunch sack hanging in her hands. She glanced up at me, then lowered her eyes and turned to head off across the parking lot.

I sighed, and the air smelled like horses. My hiccups had stopped. I hadn't noticed when.

At the end of Bible School every day the curb in front of the church was lined with station wagons, with the motors all going so you felt it under your skin. When the car doors opened, you would smell the moms' perfume and their cigarettes. The kids would climb in, safe in there, a complete small world inside, shutting the doors behind them.

I walked down the sidewalk alone, and a car door swung back open. A girl leaned her head out, one of the Devotions, named Ellen. "Mia, do you need a ride someplace?"

I looked in at the tidy car, the radio playing, her mom's fingers with a diamond ring, resting on the steering wheel, and I wanted it, but something held me back. It wasn't mine. I needed my own.

"No, thank you. That's okay. I live close."

"Bye, then," Ellen said. "See you tomorrow." She pulled the door shut, and the car nosed out from the curb. I waved into the blue cloud of exhaust.

"One of your new best friends?"

Sinclair stood behind me, hands on her hips. Her elbows angled out like arrowheads. I didn't answer.

"Well, I hope you'll be very happy," she said, "just cheerleading and discussing eyelash curlers and looking down your nose at anybody who doesn't care about those things."

"It's not like that, Sinclair," I said. "You don't know."

"No. You don't know." Sinclair reached over one shoulder and scratched violently at her back. "I'm the one who's lived here all my life and gone to school with them and seen what they're really like, how boring and snobby and useless they are. I'm the one who knows!"

"Well, you're the one who sounds snobby right now."

We stood, facing each other. Overhead the clouds were

cracking apart, allowing weak stripes of light to touch the pavement around us. Sinclair lifted the bottom of her shirt and scratched underneath.

"It looks disgusting when you do that, you know."

"Yeah. Well, that sounds like something that one of Corinne Hilt's friends would think."

"Sinclair, I don't have to be a weirdo just because you are. The way you've been acting! You really think you are a saint!"

"No." Sinclair shook her head slowly. "I know I'm not. But, see, I thought you were."

She turned and limped down the sidewalk, not looking back. Her shoulders had their familiar droop; her hair poked out as crazily as always.

I watched her hobble through a shaft of sunlight and then beyond it. It would be nothing, so easy, to run and catch up with her, to get things back the way they'd been. But I stood there. Cicadas sang out in the drying tree branches. I made the choice. I let her go.

C H A P T E R

17

Being with the Devotions could keep you safe; that was the best thing. Every day you knew what to wear because Ellen or Cathy or one of them would call to let you know: print shorts or plain, T-shirt or blouse, no need to guess. At lunchtimes, when I escaped Mrs. Wilmott's group, I could blend right in with the Devotions, belonging. We had power that way, just showing we belonged. I loved every part, linking arms and being carried off with them, letting them teach me the right things: Nice girls didn't wear red nail polish under age sixteen; when you got a boyfriend, you shouldn't let him give you a hickey, that looked cheap; and, if you were brought up right, you answered "yes, ma'am" or "yes, sir" when you talked to adults unless they were colored.

"What do you like to do for fun, Mia?" Corinne asked. Everybody stopped talking when she spoke. If she complained of the heat, everybody tried to be the first one to fold her a fan out of a napkin. Now they all waited for me to answer her. I thought fast, rejecting my paper dolls as a topic, wondering if I could dare to talk about the book of poems, how once you started opening up the words of the poetry you didn't stop. You went on, finding out more and more. "Colour-deaf," I would repeat aloud in my bed at night. "Clinker-built." It went beyond the letters, past any dictionary meaning. It was the sound and the shape of the word in your mouth and where your eyes hit it on the page. *Purple, a little, the bloom, like musty chocolate.* When it was right, you felt it in some deep unknown part of yourself. That was the thrill.

I looked around at the circle of Devotions, at how they sat politely, their smooth faces tipped, waiting.

"Miniature golf," I said finally. "I like that."

After Bible School we went downtown all together, to Bennie's, where the walls were decorated with 45 rpm records hung on nails and pennants from Tennessee colleges. Everybody filling the booths was just around our age, shooting straw papers and unwrapping the sugar cubes to suck on. The waitress, Tara, didn't get bothered by what we did. She loaded her tray with glasses of Coke and stepped over the feet sticking out of the booths, unfazed by straw wrappers flying by. She was very pretty with piled blond hair and small babylike features, and she was also the inspiration for one of the Devotions' rules because of the brilliant hickeys that were displayed like rubies on her thin, fine neck.

I sat there, savoring everything, the syrupy Coke; the small, unnaturally clear chips of ice that you could crunch in your teeth when the drink was all gone; just being there, squeezed into the booth with all the others. When one of us had something to tell, she leaned forward, over the table, and then we all would lean in, heads nearly touching, breathing our special air.

I walked home from Bennie's, and I knew my way around all the streets now. I knew the smell of the ginkgo trees in front of the dentist's office and just where to expect the barking collie dog to rush out as I passed by. When you had been reading poems, everything you saw began to seem like a part of a poem, and that was how the scenery of Ionia was that day. The rusty wheelbarrow left in somebody's side lot. The flecks of mica glittering in the sidewalk. Even the collie dog with his matted fur and little raisinlike eyes. Poetry!

I spread my arms as if I could gather it all in. I skipped across Kit's yard and up the steps, and there, in the porch swing, sat my sisters.

"Déjà vu," Nell said, putting down her French magazine to look at me.

"Surprise, surprise," Bibi said.

Their same haughty voices. They were really here. I flew at them, landing sprawled across their laps, sending the porch swing lurching crazily.

"Ouch. Mia! Honestly." But they touched my face, smoothing my long bangs backs from my eyes and pulled me in next to them, holding on. I felt their warm skin, smelled the French soap they washed with, tiny cakes made from marigold petals that they would never let me use. They were really here at last. I slumped back happily against them.

"You're suffocating me," Nell complained. They both slid sideways then, making room for me in between them, just where I wanted to be.

"I didn't know you were coming," I said.

"Gee, you should have asked," Bibi said. "In one of the many letters you wrote."

"If it's inconvenient, we can always leave," Nell said. "If it's interrupting your busy schedule." *Shed-jule,* she pronounced it.

I looked back and forth, from one to the other. Nell had new round glasses that circled her eyes like a raccoon's rings. Bibi's hair had grown longer, and she wore it a different way, pulled into a thick braid the color of caramel. They never sunbathed, and their high, pale foreheads were like something you saw in portraits, in museums. They weren't like anybody else, but I didn't care just then. They were here, and they were mine.

"Stay," I told them. "Don't ever go away from me again."

I needed to go to the bathroom, but I thought, What if they're not here when I come back? What if I'm dreaming it all up? I pressed my knees together and shivered.

The screen door squeaked open, and my aunt appeared. She had recently decided to paint her dingy casts, and now they were a vivid yellow, the same color as the stripe down the center of the highway. She had also taken to wearing long scarves, knotted at her throat. Today she had on two, gauzy shades of green, twisted together, the ends trailing like bands of seaweed over her shoulders.

"Oh, Mia, you're home," she said. "Well, what about all this?" She nodded toward my sisters. "How's this for a big surprise?"

Before I could answer, the door squeaked again. A man stepped onto the porch, and I smiled because I recognized him even though I didn't know who he was. In Ohio one time Miss Hoffmeyer's boyfriend came to the door of the classroom. "Boys and girls, this is my beau," she told us, and we all grinned, confused, because he was the weather man from the TV news. This felt the same. I squinted at the man, trying to place him, his sandy brown hair and long, boyish face.

"Mia," Kit said, "I don't think you've ever met Morse, your—Well, let's see, he would be your—You know, he's Bibi and Nell's dad. Morse."

That was it then. The snapshots from my sisters' bedroom. Morse Cooper. Of course. In the glow of having my sisters back, I hadn't even considered how they'd gotten here, who had brought them. Morse Cooper. The stain that kept our family from ever being a regular family.

"Mia," he said now. He stepped forward and stuck out his hand.

Everybody was watching, so I shook it, looking down.

He was wearing sneakers, and he had big feet. Even this was more information than I needed about him. I didn't care to know the details, I was just ready to have him go, back the way he came, leaving my sisters with me, where they belonged. I turned then and spotted the car, parked in the driveway where I hadn't noticed it before, a dusty wood-paneled station wagon, with suitcases and boxes piled in the back.

"We're going to take a little walk," Kit said. "Morse wants to see Ionia again. He hasn't been back here in all these years."

"I'm afraid you'll find it unchanged, Morse," Bibi said, "still a wasteland."

So they called him Morse, not Dad. I gazed out at the catalpa tree. I didn't care what they called him. I didn't need to know. His hand had felt warm and slightly rough against mine. It was a hand that had once touched my mom. I looked down again, digging my fingernails into my palms.

"Well, it's all right with me if it's unchanged," Morse Cooper said as he and my aunt started down the porch steps. "I liked it fine twenty years ago."

"*Chacun à son goût!*" Nell yelled after him.

"Sure, Tippecanoe and Tyler, too," he called back.

We sat still in the swing until they had crossed the yard and headed along the sidewalk. Then both my sisters turned to me, talking at the same time.

"What's with Kit?"

"She was such a mouse when we left here!"

"And now look at her! I almost didn't recognize her."

"What did you *do* to her, Mia?"

"Nothing," I said. "Except, you know, when I broke her arms that time."

"Well, I don't understand it, but it's an improvement, I'd say," Nell said.

"She looks kind of dashing, really," Bibi said.

We all stared down the street at my aunt swinging her blazing yellow casts as she walked, her foamy scarves floating out behind her.

"You probably can't tell," I announced shyly, "but I've changed, too. I'm friends with these girls now at Bible School, and they're teaching me how to do cheerleading and everything."

"Oh, spare me," Nell said, standing up. "I don't think I can stomach the gory details of the cheerleading life in Ionia, Tennessee."

"Moi, non plus." Bibi stretched her arms and stood up, too. "That was a long drive. I'm going to take a shower."

"Wait!" I was alone on the swing. I could feel the empty spaces on either side. "I wanted to tell you. I also like poems now. I read them every night."

"Poems? Really?" They stood, looking at me, their eyebrows lifted. Their faces were long, shaped just like Morse Cooper's. I didn't want to see it, but I had to. I didn't have anybody who only belonged to me.

"Edna St. Vincent Millay," I pronounced carefully. The name was a poem by itself.

"Oh. *Millay*. Well." Bibi gave a small shrug.

"What?" I said. "What about her?"

Bibi shrugged again. "She's all right. A lot of people like her work. It's just that, for my taste, she's a trifle sentimental."

"And obvious," Nell said. "If you really hope to tackle poetry, Mia, you'll want to take on some more challenging poets. Yeats. Auden. We can make you a list."

"Yes," Bibi said. "We'll make you a complete list."

"No, thanks." They looked so affronted it made me laugh, and then, suddenly, I was desperate. I couldn't hold it any longer.

I leaped out of the swing and ran around back, behind the metal toolshed. I pulled down my pants and crouched, careful not to wet on my shorts. I loved Edna St. Vincent Millay, and if they didn't, she could be all mine. My sisters were really back, already trying to boss me again. I finished peeing and took a long, hard breath, pure relief.

18

In the morning Morse Cooper was still there. It seemed that the only people who ever went away were the ones I wanted to keep with me. The house felt different with a man staying there. I threw butter into the hot iron skillet and pushed it around with a fork. His heavy footsteps overhead made the dishes rattle on the shelves. He had slept on the cot in the attic room, and I hoped he had found it stifling and so inhospitable that he would want to hurry right back to his own bed in his own town, hundreds of miles away.

I cracked eggs into the pan and stirred them. It was Saturday, so there was no Bible School, just a free day. And now, with Bibi and Nell here, it seemed like a day with promise. I turned off the flame and put the steaming eggs on my plate. I poured a glass of milk since Saturday was one of the days I could allow myself to drink it, obeying the orders from the air.

In Beirut I used to dream the flat, plain taste of milk. We only had powdered there. You mixed it in pitchers, and it came out different thicknesses each time, always too sweet. It stuck on your tongue. The kids I knew there just thought that was how milk was. In Scouts, once, they took us out on a motor launch to go aboard an American aircraft carrier called the *Forrestal* that was anchored in the harbor. After they had shown us the engine room and the bunks and all the airplanes chained to the deck, they took us to the dining hall to give us cookies and glasses of milk. It was the regular milk that I had been dreaming about, brought from the States, and I took the tiniest sips I could, to keep it, to make it real. Everybody wanted me to finish. The motor launch was waiting. Finally, the cook with the sailor hat poured the milk into a Dixie cup for me to take, but on the launch the wind lifted it out of my hands, and then it was gone, like something I only dreamed after all.

Now I sat down at the table, my plate and my glass in front of me, just right. I liked the minute when the food was on the table, before you took a bite, and how the kitchen was, so still, before everybody else would come in to fill it up, spreading the newspaper out and making the teakettle whistle. I sighed happily and stuck my fork into my eggs. Almost instantly I heard him thumping down the stairs from the attic. He was whistling. I started to pick up my dishes, but there wasn't time to escape to the porch. The door opened, and there he was.

"Hello, Mia."

"Hi." I stared at my plate, chopping the eggs into bits with the side of my fork.

"That smells good," he said. "Eggs."

I didn't answer, since there wasn't anything to say. He pulled out a chair and sat down, across from me, the table empty in front of him. I wondered if he was thinking I would fix him food and set him a place.

"There's more eggs in the icebox," I said finally. "You can use the same pan."

"Thanks," he said. "I'll probably cook some later, after I take a walk."

"A walk?" I couldn't keep the dismay out of my voice. How long was he going to stick around, putting off his departure, intruding on our day? "I mean, Ionia's not that big," I said. "You probably saw enough of it when you walked around yesterday."

"Oh, no," he said. "Not enough."

If he had been somebody else, I would have offered to go along, to show him the best things: the silty creeks and the ginkgo trees and the surprise of the vacant lot on French Street, glowing with butterweed in full bloom. I pushed my eggs around, and that was the only sound for a few minutes, the fork scraping on the plate.

Morse Cooper stood up. He was tall, but not so tall as my dad, not so long-boned, no thin, royal nose. "Want to come along?" he said.

I shook my head.

"There's so much I had forgotten about here," he said. "The blue chicory everywhere. The way it sprouts up in the ditches, along the highway, even between cracks in the pavement. The clover fields. I had forgotten that clover has its own peculiar smell that you can't describe, except that it smells green. And even the constant hum of the cement plant. Pretty quickly that becomes as familiar to you as the sound of your own breathing."

"And the creeks!" I said excitedly, not thinking. "You have to go see the creeks, too."

"Are you sure you don't want to come along?"

I sat back, remembering then. My sisters' father, what an odd idea. There wasn't even a name for what relation he would be to me. Just nothing.

"No, sir," I said. "I don't."

After he left, Kit poked her head into the kitchen, looking around. Her dress needed zipping. "I thought I heard Morse's voice," she said.

"Umhmm. He went for a walk."

She stepped into the room and turned for me to work the zipper. "Did he have something to eat first? Did you make him some eggs?"

I shrugged, watching her freckled back disappear as the two panels of fabric joined. "He said he would fix his own."

"Oh, Mia, you know that was just being polite. He's our guest."

"How long is he staying anyhow?"

"Awhile, I reckon," Kit said. She walked over and snapped on the flame under the teakettle. "I know. Maybe I'll make waffles to have ready when he gets back. We used to have a waffle iron. I'm sure it's still around somewhere."

"But how long is awhile?" I said. "You mean, a few days?"

"I mean awhile, that's all." Kit opened a cupboard door and squatted down, sliding things around. She slammed the door shut and stepped sideways to the next cupboard. "Aha, here it is!"

"Not weeks," I said. "It doesn't mean weeks."

Kit backed out of the cupboard. "Mia, quit it," she said. "Run along now, and say 'get up' to your sleepyhead sisters. Say I'm making waffles for everybody."

Nell trimmed my hair out in the backyard. I stood still, and she held my bangs out in the vee of her fingers, the way she would hold a cigarette. I closed my eyes each time she lifted the scissors, but I liked the sensation of the blades cutting. My hair seemed to buzz.

Bibi sat nearby, in the grass, squinting up, offering advice. "More on the left, Nell. Over just a fraction. Yes, there."

"The shape of your face has changed this summer," Nell told me. "You're getting cheekbones." She touched my face lightly with the point of the scissors.

"And hips," Bibi said. "You're beginning to get those, too."

"I am?" I squirmed, delighted, prodding my hipbones, which certainly did seem rounder under my shorts.

"Hold still now," Nell said, so sweetly that I was suddenly alert. Something wasn't right. Something loomed underneath all this, the sunshine in the backyard, the careful snip of the scissors, the doting big sisters.

"What do you do to get a hickey?" I asked quickly, to distract them from whatever they were leading up to.

Bibi's hand flew up to her smooth neck. "Not very much." She touched there, smiling. "Find any boy with a mouth. He'll do the rest."

"You can take her word for it," Nell said. "She speaks from experience."

"And *you* don't?" Bibi said. "Dare I mention those sailors from the USS *Essex*?"

"Okay. If *I* can mention one Monsieur Desloges, *un vrai professeur de l'amour, n'est-ce pas?*"

"I *told* you, he was just tutoring me. In declensions." Bibi touched her neck again. She looked up at Nell, and they both began to laugh.

"Ah, declensions!" Nell thrust her arm up high in the air. The scissors blades flashed in the sunlight. "Long may they require tutorials!"

The screen door smacked shut, and Kit walked slowly toward us, frowning at a piece of paper in her hand.

"The oddest thing," she said. "Mia, do you have *any* idea why there are half a dozen calls to Washington, D.C., on the phone bill?"

My skin burned, and I felt the hair clippings sting like

nettles down my collar. There wouldn't be any use lying. Just to look at the color of my face, they would know.

"I had to call Mr. Burton, you know, that government guy."

"To say what?"

I sighed, peering up at the sky. Sometimes it was so blue and endless it frightened me. "I didn't say anything. I don't know. It's because he's the one who's searching. See, I just wanted to hear a voice."

Everything was quiet except for the neighbor's sprinkler slapping water against the wooden fence each time it pivoted in our direction. My aunt stood still, staring down at the telephone bill as if she could make herself understand that way.

"I'll pay you back," I said, not meaning it. I knew she would say I didn't need to pay. I knew how it touched grown-ups, the idea of kids giving out their nickels and dimes. I hung my head down, sucking in my cheeks. My hair clippings lay all around, nearly the color of the dry grass but shinier.

"You don't have to pay me, honey!" Kit said. She turned to my sisters then, shaking her head. "For God's sake," she said to them, "let's don't put this off any longer."

"All right, *all right*," Bibi said. "We were just going to tell her anyhow."

"Right when you came outside," Nell said. "We were about to."

"Well, you've had twenty-four hours," Kit said. "You've been here that long."

"What?" I said. They wouldn't look at me. I shivered in the bright sunshine. "Oh, never mind," I said, shivering. "Never mind."

"Mia," Nell said, too gently.

I thought my heart would crack. I pressed my hands over it. "Never mind!" I cried again.

"Sweetie, they've stopped searching. They had to give up. Mr. Burton called us in Boston, and we thought we'd better come here to tell you."

"Shut up. I can't even hear you!" I stuck my fingers in my ears. "Shut up."

Bibi got up from the grass, and her face was crumpled. A mask of woe. She stepped toward me, holding out her arms. I leaned over and swooped up the scissors Nell had dropped.

"I'll stab you." I shut my eyes and thrust wildly, blindly at the air. "Get back or I'll stab you all!"

A hand clamped my wrist, making the scissors fall. I opened my eyes, and it was Morse Cooper, there from nowhere.

"Whoa," he said. "No injuries. We don't need that now."

I leaned forward and bit into his knuckle as deep as I could go, feeling my teeth slice through.

He gave a low cry, and then I was free. I pushed right past them, their row of stunned white faces. I ran down the sidewalk, around the corner, I didn't notice where. Everything was salt then, the tears washing down my face, the taste of blood on my tongue, that Dixie cup of milk, dissolved into the sea. I cried harder then. It wasn't fair. How long I'd hoped for those sips of milk.

CHAPTER

19

After that was when I started to steal things. I went
into other kids' lunch bags and took the two cookies that
somebody had carefully wrapped in wax paper or the
hard-boiled egg or sometimes even the main thing, the
sandwich with the crusts trimmed off. I took one or two
bites and tossed it out, in the trash barrel. Sometimes
there was money in the lunch sack, sometimes a note
from the mom saying: "Remember, I'll pick you up to
take you to your piano lesson. XXX." I took these, too,
and threw them away. Pretty soon they sent a notice
home for the parents saying how sorry they were to
report that there was an unknown thief at the Bible
School. I threw that out, too. I didn't have parents.

"Really, Mia, it's only that they've called off the official
search," Nell told me. "That's all. Nothing more."

"That's all," Bibi repeated.

It was dark in my room. I couldn't see their faces, only their short white nightgowns and the outline of their bodies. They had come in and sat down on the edge of my bed, pinning me there beneath the tight sheet to get me to listen.

I slithered down to the end of the bed, hiding my head under the covers until they went away. Anyhow, I knew. I always knew. If nobody searched, if nobody went and made them turn back, she would keep going. She would sail on and on, just on and on. You could know that by the light in her eyes when she stared at the stars. Sky, sea, it was all the same. She was always waiting to go. I wrote this down to send to Mr. Burton to make him understand, to get him out hunting again. But there on paper it looked like something you would never say about a mother. I threw the letter away, too.

Morse Cooper couldn't drive back to Boston now, with his hand swollen and bandaged. He'd been treated at the emergency room, where they'd given him an injection of antibiotics and a ten-day supply of penicillin.

"The danger is septicemia, of course," Nell said, "especially in this heat. A human bite is really dirty. Dirtier than a dog bite even."

"God, poor Morse," Bibi said. "Now how's he going to get his writing done?"

"I don't know," Nell said. "And we made him drive us down here."

"Well, he wanted to come."

"God knows why. This godforsaken place."

I looked up from the Honey Bunch book I was pretending to read. "He likes it here," I said in a shaking voice. "He thinks it's pretty."

The day was so hot you could feel a film all over your skin. You could crunch the grit from the cement plant between your teeth. My sisters turned toward me with flushed, disagreeable faces.

"You honestly believe he still likes it here? After what you've put him through?"

"Have you even apologized to him for what you did?"

"God, Mia. The way you act! You're not the only one who's upset, you know. You can't do these things! This makes two people you've sent to the hospital in one summer."

Three, I corrected silently. I looked back down at the book, watching tears start to splat down on goody-goody Honey Bunch. Three people, if you counted me.

I stole Nell's tortoiseshell compact and kept it in my bureau drawer. I liked to open it just to touch the disk of hard powder inside and watch my fingertips go pink. My haircut had never been finished, and it stayed that way, in ragged layers around my neck. Nobody showed any interest in fixing it, and I wasn't going to ask them. I wouldn't ask for anything, not now. I could just take what I needed.

Hatty came by with more maps for Kit.

"Well, okay. You can leave these," my aunt said. "But that's it. These are the last ones I'm going to do."

"Phoo," Hatty said. "You know you're not going to quit."

"Just watch me. I might. I probably will."

I was on the sofa, my legs folded under me, picking the scab on a mosquito bite.

"Mia," Hatty called, "I didn't bring any paper dolls today, but I have another idea. How would you like to get out of here for a little while? I was thinking this might be a good time for you to come see my place. You can finally meet my kitty-cats."

I looked up in time to see my aunt nodding emphatically yes at Hatty and shaping the words *thank you, thank you, thank you* with her mouth.

"No, thank you." I resumed chipping at the scab. "Maybe some other time."

There was silence. Hatty swung her big face around, finding her purse. "Well, sure," she said after a minute. "I'll give you a raincheck then. Sure." She said it "shirr," the same as my mom did, the same as Kit, too.

My mom always told how she took almost nothing from Ionia when she left, just a suitcase of high school girl clothes that she got rid of as soon as she could afford new ones. But now, after living here, I saw. She had taken things she didn't even know. Certain words she used for everyday objects—washrag, scrap basket, ink pen—were what they all said here. And the shape of her handwriting, the tilted loops on the *L*'s, the way the *M*'s sprawled wide like flying birds, was from the method they taught in the Ionia school. I saw it again and again when the girls passed notes at Bible camp or even when Tara, the waitress at Bennie's, wrote down our orders on her lined pad. Wherever my mom was, how far away she could ever get, she would still carry those things, Ionia things. So ha-ha on her, I thought.

After Hatty left, Kit sat down next to me on the sofa. "I think that would have done you good," she said. "A change of scene, going over to Hatty's."

I shrugged.

"She even has a pool there at her apartment complex. You could have gone for a swim."

I stopped working at my scab. A pool. Just to jump into chilled, chlorinated water with the sunlight bouncing off the surface and swim, parting the water with cupped hands, forgetting anything else. "How come she didn't say that then? That she has a pool?"

"Well, she shouldn't have to *bribe* you to get you there," Kit said. She sighed. "I don't know, Mia, I don't know. You and I have been through a lot already this summer, and really we're just starting out. It's going to go on from here." She laced her fingertips together. Her casts were like bright stripes crossing her lap. "Well, I'm not like Jess. I never can be. I knew that from the time I was three years old probably. But we have to figure all this out somehow, don't we? How to live?"

It was so tempting to say yes, to just give in. It would be the same as jumping into the pool and floating, letting the natural forces take over, the easiest thing. Buoyancy. I knew how my dad would name it and explain it, how he'd understand it.

"No," I told her. "No! Quit nagging me, why don't you?" I got up and walked through the house back to my room, where a blast of thick heat hit me when I opened the door. I sat on my bed in the sweltering air, turning the limp pages of the poem book and sniffling.

After a while I took out the stolen compact and flicked it open. What I saw in the mirror wasn't surprising. The runny nose, the chopped, sweaty hair, my bangs sloping up my forehead like a hem sewn crooked. I looked like what I knew I was, somebody's abandoned child.

CHAPTER

20

"How come you wear those baby shoes?" I said. "Does your mom make you wear those?"

The girl I was talking to, Taffy, looked down at her feet. She was in the Devotions, but she was younger, just on the outer edge, always smiling, grateful to be included. Her blouses had lace collars, perfectly ironed, and often she had a lipstick outline on her cheek from being kissed good-bye. Now everybody looked at her round-toed buckle shoes.

"I used to wear those, too," I said. "When I was about four years old."

With the Devotions I could act as mean as I wanted. They liked if you were mean, as long as you did it right. Nobody said it, but you saw how it worked. For instance, you would never do it to a teacher or any other grown-up. With them you just gave a compliment to their ugliest thing: Mrs. Wilmott, I *love* your dress, that mustard color looks so pretty on you. And you would never do it to somebody you had to truly be sorry for—the kids who'd had polio and came to Bible School twice a week on a special bus. When they arrived at Bible camp, stepping stiffly down from the bus, with their metal leg braces creaking, the Devotions just acted nice about it. They said "hey" to them as if they were the same as anybody.

You could only be mean to somebody who was almost all right, just a little bit off. You found the one thing about them that was soft or wrong, and you said it out loud. I was getting so good at it I was moving higher up in the Devotions. They saved me a sought-after shady seat at the next lunchtime.

Taffy came running over and said, "Guess what, Mia, my mama's taking me to buy nice shoes after Bible School this afternoon!"

"You really ought to wash your cheek," I told her. "You have lip marks there."

Ellen and Marybeth and a couple of others always sat around me. They hunted in their lunches for something good to share. Sometimes I had already been through their lunch sacks, stashed with all the others in the cubbyholes in the church basement. I didn't take things from Devotions usually. I just wanted to know what they had. As we sat there, I could have named each thing before they unwrapped it: tuna sandwich, dill pickle, vanilla wafers. They would never guess.

Only Corinne made me nervous. She watched me when the others were grouped around me, as if she were close to knowing something, just waiting to figure it out. Her eyes blinked, like a camera click. I looked down, guarding my secrets.

The first person to catch me stealing was a fat boy from Mr. Wilmott's group. He came out of the rest room so fast, still pulling up his zipper, and there I was, squatting in front of the cubbyholes, my hand deep inside a paper sack. He saw me, and his mouth went flat. He walked right past me and out through the door. My face flamed. I threw the lunch bag down. The prissy way he had pressed lips together, judging me. The Devotions would never even *look* at you, I wanted to tell him. You don't even take the time to wash your hands after the bathroom.

I was certain he would tell on me. For the rest of the day I waited for the tap on the shoulder or the sound of heavy footsteps as Mr. Wilmott and Mrs. Carter approached, like a posse to lead me away. My face burned, feverish all afternoon, anticipating the shame. When nothing happened, I felt so light and lucky I swore over and over to myself that I wouldn't do it again.

I didn't, for a day or two. Then Mrs. Wilmott sent me inside with a can of paintbrushes to be rinsed, and when I passed the cubbies, they drew me right over. All those bags. It wasn't the food; it was something else. I wanted what they had. I started pulling bags off the shelves and digging inside, and this time the one who caught me was Sinclair.

She had followed me in with more paintbrushes, and now she stood still in the corridor, letting them drip into her cupped hand. "Well, I knew it was you," she said quietly. "All along I knew."

"No, it's not," I said. "I'm just putting these lunches back. I found them all pulled out of the cubbyholes. I found them that way, and I thought I should put them back."

"Oh, come on," Sinclair said. "Don't bother to lie about it."

"I'm not lying!"

"And that's another lie. Should I start keeping count?"

We stood facing each other in the dim basement. The paint was leaking out, in muddy drips between her fingers. We had spent the morning in Mrs. Wilmott's group, making illustrations of the Holy Land from descriptions in the Bible. Chalky hillsides, rainbows, burning bushes, olive trees. The kids who'd painted olives growing in the trees made them just how they'd always seen them in the jar, drab green with a bright pimiento in each.

"Those brushes are dripping all over your tennis shoes," I said.

"You take them then." Sinclair stepped forward and deposited them in the can next to me. "You're the one that's supposed to be cleaning them. I just came in to see if that's what you really were doing."

"So, what are you going to do now? Tell on me?"

Sinclair gave me a disdainful look. "Why would I tell? Who cares about lunches? I just wanted to know for myself. Now I do know." She wiped her messy hands on her shorts and headed for the door.

"Yeah, little Miss Sainthood who steals books out of the library!"

Sinclair paused in the open doorway. "Actually, I returned that book if you really want to know," she said.

"Huh, I mean the *saint* book that you tore the card pocket right out of."

"I know," Sinclair said. "That one. I gave it back to the library. They just glue another card thing in."

"You did not," I said. "You wouldn't ever give that book back."

"Why wouldn't I? I don't need it anymore. I'm done being a saint. I have new things to do. Better things." She shrugged. "Anyway, go down and look on the library shelf if you don't believe me."

I felt a stab of longing. What new things? Suddenly I just wanted to be back in her room on the sky blue rug, planning everything over again. I was weary of trying to be regular, to fit in. I was the only one at camp who'd walked in a real olive grove. I was the one who knew how the trees really looked, but I hadn't dared tell it. What I saw just now was how it turned out, again and again, that the things that made you happiest were the very same things that kept you from ever fitting in. The hours on the blue rug. The too-sweet smell of the tiny olive flowers and how you could run through the grove and feel the leathery leaves tap your skin. You shouldn't just trade those things away.

"Oh, Sinclair," I cried, "I don't know what to do. They're gone. They're gone. They're not coming back."

But the door had already clicked shut. She was gone, too.

I walked home, thinking everything over, listing how I would change: I'd call up Sinclair, never steal another thing. I'd be nice to people no matter what. The sun warmed the top of my head. I felt almost melted with goodness. It was so easy. Everybody should just be kind and honest and good.

I skipped up the front walk. My sisters were on the porch reading as usual.

"Hey," I greeted them. They were eating penuche out of a pan placed between them on the swing. "Can I have some?"

"*May* I have some," Nell corrected, not looking up from her book.

"Okay. May I have some?"

"Did you say please?"

"Please."

"Please what?"

"*Please* may I have some penuche."

"No." They looked at each other and laughed.

Always there were two of them, one of me. I decided

to start spreading my new goodness somewhere else. "Where's Kit?" I asked.

Bibi lifted one sticky hand and gestured toward the house. "Wait, though, Mia, I will cut you a piece of the penuche."

"Oh, no," I said sweetly. "It's all yours."

I found my aunt sitting, cross-legged, on the living room floor, surrounded by tubes and wires from the television set. She had on blue jeans that looked brand-new, and her hair was up in a tiny ponytail. Morse Cooper had his head deep inside the open back of the TV cabinet and was tapping at things with the tip of a screwdriver.

"We have this whole television in pieces!" my aunt announced to me, unnecessarily. She was barefoot, and so was he. I saw the big pale soles of his feet as he knelt there. They seemed like something private. I hung back, standing outside the door to the room.

"Morse knows how to get things working right again!" Kit said, smiling at his back. Her toes were almost touching his. Her casts were newly painted, fire engine red. "I think we'll have it going by tonight."

Nice, I reminded myself fiercely, nice no matter what.

Morse Cooper eased back out of the television and turned around. The front of his shirt was streaked with red paint. "I just need one new fuse," he said. "Then we can try it out."

"Just one little fuse?" Kit said happily. "That's it? I knew you'd do it, Morse! See, you *do* have the magic touch." She turned to me, making her silly ponytail flutter. "Did you hear that, Mia? One little fuse and—voilà—*Bonanza*. Or, I don't know, is *Bonanza* still on the air? How about *77 Sunset Strip*? I just know the old programs. I'll have to learn the new! So, what do you say, honey?" She gave me a wide smile. "What would you recommend?"

"You should put your shoes back on," I said coldly.

I fled then, out the screen door and across the porch, stopping only to snatch the pan of penuche out from between my sisters' knees. I ran down the road and pushed through the sumac in the vacant lot to reach the edge of the creek. I sat in the tall grass with the pan in my lap. Already the sweetness of the stolen penuche seemed more rewarding than goodness ever could be. I ate until my teeth ached.

CHAPTER
21

Things got worse. We began to have real dinners, every-body around the table, candlelight flickering across the faces, as if we were supposed to be a regular family. I had to look down and touch where my heart was, still beating, under my blouse. Stop, I ordered it. But it went on. I couldn't stand that things just went on the same as ever: hearts beating, candles shining, the steam rising up from the food. All around me they were talking, talking.

"He's going to go through with it. He said on the news. He's going to be the first Negro at that university no matter what they do to stop him."

"Well, they better not think they can stop him. It's a court order. He's going to have armed troops there to protect him."

"Oh, they don't care about that; they'll try anything. Look at how they burn down churches!"

"Well, I would just love to go right down there to Mississippi and cheer him on. I think he's so brave. I think he's a hero."

"It's not even that far. We could get there on a train, I bet."

"Let's find out! We should go down there. I'll call the bus station and—"

"Wait one minute. Hold everything. It's a noble cause, but I am not letting the two of you go down there into the thick of all that trouble."

"Oh, Morse, really! I *am* practically eighteen years old."

"And I certainly know how to take care of myself. Remember, I won the fencing prize at the lycée. Also, all my ballet training! Madame told us that even prizefighters study ballet to strengthen their muscles and improve their technique."

I poked my food with my fork. Four more bites, then I could ask to be excused. It was something Bibi and Nell had cooked. "Oh, shepherd's pie!" Kit said when she came to the table, but they insisted that it was a dish called *boeuf parmentier*. I would have called it hash. I touched above my heart again. It ticked stubbornly. Just on and on.

Morse Cooper's bandages were gone now, and there was only a curved red scar. I didn't look at him if I could help it. I never said his name. In the evenings, just before dinner, when they all gathered to watch the Huntley-

Brinkley news show, I stayed away, working on my collection of deformed paper dolls. No matter how much I would have liked to glimpse Caroline Kennedy or hear the Alka-Seltzer song again, I stayed away. I wouldn't watch the television that he had repaired.

I ate my last forkful.

"I've been reading all about a cave near here." Now he was speaking. I didn't look. I drained my water glass and wiped my mouth with the back of my hand.

"Mia," Nell said, "you do have a napkin."

"Snail Shell Cave, it's called."

"Oh, sure, I've been there," Kit said. "We used to go sometimes when we were kids."

"The guidebook said they've identified nearly twenty separate varieties of snails there, in that one cave."

"Uh-huh, well, there are plenty all right." Kit made a face. "I remember the big ones didn't just have antennae; they had *antlers*. I mean it! And if you shone your flashlight on the walls, you saw the trails they left behind, all those crisscrossed snail tracks just glistening all over the walls."

I sat forward in my chair. I could just taste the cool chalk air of a cave. I could already see the maze of dazzling tracks against the dark stone, like a huge, mysterious painting.

"Well, I want to go over and have a look," Morse said. "Also, it's supposed to be a good spot for finding crystals and even whole geodes. I thought I might just drive over there tomorrow afternoon. Anybody interested in coming along?"

Crystals, too. I shut my eyes. Oh, go, go, I begged everybody silently. If they all went, then I could go, too, just one of the passengers, along for the ride. It wasn't the same as accepting his invitation. It wasn't saying yes.

"Well, I can't tomorrow," Kit said. "I have a map deadline. Hatty's coming by at four o'clock."

"And I'm not much of one for spelunking," Nell said. "Even in the interest of science. I get too claustrophobic."

"You can just bring me back a geode, Morse," Bibi said, "but no snails, thank you."

I stood up before they could turn to me for my answer. Already my untrustworthy heart was beating: Say yes, say yes. "Please may I be excused?" I said instead, holding out my empty plate.

Outside, the air felt thinner. The nights lasted longer. Summer was ending, and in a few weeks school would start. School in America. What I had longed for and cried to my mom about. Now I would have it. I sighed and kicked at the gravel in the driveway, making it spray into the grass. The next time Morse Cooper mowed, he would have to squat down and pluck the stones back out of the lawn, one by one. I kicked again.

Just ahead of me was the narrow space between the garage and the wooden fence. It wasn't night yet. There was still the low, gloomy light of the end of the day, but in that thin space it was already black, the deepest black that could swallow you. I shivered, already knowing. The command was coming.

It came. Go in there. Go on in that space.

I had to. You didn't argue. You didn't bargain. I turned sideways and squeezed through the narrow opening. Cobwebs were everywhere. I pushed them away from my face, and they stuck to my fingers. The darkness was like a cloth thrown over your head. You could feel its weight. More than anything I wanted to move my eyes, to look back out at the everyday world with its fading light and the smell of fried meat from the houses and the dull clatter of the dinner pans being scrubbed in the sinks. But it wasn't allowed. Just for thinking of it, I had to move five steps deeper into the dark space, five steps farther away from the world.

I stood there, counting to a hundred. Twice I had to start over for counting too fast, for rushing through it. Something shifted in the dry leaves, some little animal, close to my feet, but I counted on. It was my only hope, just to follow these orders, the harder the better. It was what I could do. Fifty-seven. Wait. Fifty-eight. Wait. Fifty-nine. More slowly than my heart could ever beat, I counted.

"So, who cut your hair, Mia?"

My hand flew up to touch the uneven edges of my

hair. Everybody watched. My hair felt messier then, like the bottom of a worn-out broom.

"Um, the beauty parlor," I said. "They did it."

"Really." Corinne's eyes were the lightest blue, the blue you can sometimes see in snow. "Which beauty parlor?"

"Well, I forget the name. Anyway it wasn't in Ionia, so you wouldn't know about it probably. It was more out toward Nashville. Somewhere pretty close to Nashville, I think."

Corinne continued to look at me over the platters of french fries. We all were at Bennie's, in the booth where we always sat, squeezed in as usual, shoulders touching, but the girls on either side of me moved away slightly. I felt the warm spots where their shoulders had been. I couldn't be all alone again. I wouldn't. I talked faster.

"I've been meaning to tell you, Corinne, I really like your wristwatch. I like how it has roman numerals instead of just plain numbers. And I like the shape, too, that oval shape. It's pretty."

Corinne picked up one french fry and examined it. She frowned and let it drop back onto the plate. "You should definitely get a refund," she said, "if any beauty parlor did that."

The waitress, Tara, came over to remove our empty glasses and the plates of limp, leftover fries. I sank back, relieved. The danger was over; the worst moment had passed. I understood the patterns of meanness now. I would be safe. Already it was somebody else's turn. Marybeth, for the three ugly warts on the back of her hand.

I fingered my hair again covertly. I would get it fixed somehow. Not by my sisters. They weren't touching it again. I blinked then. As if I'd conjured them up, there they were. Bibi and Nell. They were walking down the sidewalk. I saw them from a distance through Bennie's big plate glass windows. You couldn't mistake them, even from far away. It was their thin, stiff shoulders, the haughty way they held their necks and how their lace-up sandals made them lift their feet as deliberately as dancers, as deep-sea divers. No, it couldn't be anybody else. I slid down low in the booth.

"Hey," the girl next to me complained. "Move your elbow. You're pushing me."

"Are y'all ordering anything more?" Tara lifted her tray. "Because you know you can't go on sitting here taking up space without—" She broke off her speech to stare out the front window. "Well, I declare, girls! The Martians must have landed."

Everybody turned to see. Bibi and Nell had stopped outside, directly in front of the window. They were looking up at something overhead. You could see everything: their kohl-rimmed eyes, their pale lipstick, Nell's odd raccoon glasses, pushed up on top of her head.

"Beatniks!" Marybeth said. "Those are beatniks."

"She's right. I saw some on the TV, and that's how they look."

"Look at their eyes, they scare me to death!"

"And you should hear. They *say* the trashiest stuff. You should have heard those beatniks on the TV. My mama said she'd like to wash their mouths out with soap."

"Look, those two are talking right now. What do they think they're doing out there?"

They were looking at an old window, probably, or a roofline. They were saying words like *mullion* and *cornice* and *facade*. I had seen them do it dozens of times, halting, just like this, in the middle of a sidewalk, anywhere, to discuss windowpanes or count the flutings on a column. Oh, why couldn't they stop to notice the other things? That people didn't wear tight black skirts downtown in the late August heat. Or fringed shawls. Or twine the laces of their sandals up high on their pale, beautiful legs.

"Maybe they aren't beatniks," I said in a small voice.

Everybody went quiet. Corinne's light eyes were on me again.

"Oh?" she said. "Well, what *are* they then, Mia? Why don't you tell us?"

The whole booth was still, waiting.

"Nothing. I don't know! How would I know? Just nothing." They taught me to knit a scarf and how to say swears in French. Night after night they still sat on my bed in their white nightgowns telling me things were going to be all right, everything would be all right. I looked out the big window now, and they were gone.

"Okay, girls," Tara said. "That show's over. Now is anybody going to order anything, or are y'all going to clear out of here?"

"Who has money?" Corinne said.

I dug into the pocket of my shorts and pulled out coins, all that I had. "I'll pay," I told them all. "I'll pay."

CHAPTER
22

"Summer in Tennessee," I wrote down. Immediately I crossed that out. Too dull. This was the sixth title I'd come up with and rejected. I was sitting in the dry grass next to the creek with a big yellow legal pad in my lap, ready to write a poem. Everything was here beside me: the low, sluggish creek water, the red, sulfurous mud, the sudden clicking of a dragonfly's wings. I could write it all down, but first I needed a title. That was always at the top of the page. That was how you started.

I flipped to the next sheet of yellow paper. "At the creek" I wrote on the top of the page. Bad, nothing. I scratched it out with such force that my pencil point tore the paper underneath. I had to flip over two pages to start again. The grass tickled my legs. I rubbed them and yawned. Nearby a stick snapped, then another one. I sat up straight. Somebody was coming, somebody walking in this direction.

In all the times I'd come down to the creek, I'd never seen anybody else here. It was my own place. Now there was somebody coming. I sat still. My skin prickled. I thought it was how a dog must feel when its fur lifts up before a fight.

Morse Cooper came through the bushes. At first he didn't see me. He was ducking his head to avoid the brambles. His big sneakers were rimmed with damp mud, and his legs were scratched from going through the bushes. You had to know the right path. I was the only one who knew. He stood, looking across the creek for a minute or two. Then he stepped over to it and squatted down to feel the water with his hand. It was what I always did first, too, put my fingers in the water.

He stood up again and turned around. There I was, just watching him. "Oh." He stepped back. "Mia. You surprised me there. I didn't expect to run into anything back here but a snapping turtle."

I sat still, suddenly conscious of the big yellow tablet, conspicuous in my lap, too big to hide anywhere. Technically it was Morse Cooper's legal pad, but he had left it by the telephone, and I needed it. He seemed to have plenty of them anyhow. Day after day he and Kit sat at the table, talking in low voices and writing things down on the yellow paper. When I found this pad, the top page was full of words and telephone numbers. "Legal guardianship?" Morse Cooper had written with his blue fountain pen, "Beirut apartment/storage." Things that were none of his business. I tore off the page and threw it away.

"So, Mia, is this Lime Creek?" he asked now.

"No." I shrugged and looked down, plucking at the tough, dry grass. I wasn't going to say anything more. Then I relented. "This one's called Jetty's Creek." I liked telling it. I liked that I knew and he needed to be told. "Lime Creek is the one over near the school."

"Jetty's. Aha. And Lime is over that way?"

"No, that way, and there's Ribbon Creek, too, that's another one." I couldn't stop now, showing what I knew. "It's the third one. It's far over there, out past the train tracks. It's the one with the beaver dams. But the creeks meet up, all three of them. They join together and run, miles and miles, across to the river."

"Ah, yeah, the river," Morse Cooper said. He sat down on the ground a few feet away from me and squinted his eyes as if he could see all the way to the Tennessee River instead of just this small creek bed that disappeared into a culvert up ahead. "I'm going to drive over there one of these days just to look at it again. It always makes me think of a poem I like by a man named T. S. Eliot. He called a river 'a strong brown god.'"

"Well, I read poems, too," I said quickly. He shouldn't think he was the only one. "I've read a whole big book by Edna St. Vincent Millay."

He nodded his head solemnly. "Good for you. That's impressive."

"And I even write poems. That's just what I was doing back here, writing one. I'm probably going to be a writer."

"I guess we'll have something in common then."

It took me a second to understand. I sucked in my breath. "*You're* a poet?"

"Well, no," he said, smiling. "I can't claim anything close to that, but I am a writer. A kind of writer anyway. My training is in engineering, so I write technical information. For textbooks and training manuals. I write about armored cable and thin-wall conduit, things like that."

"Oh," I said.

He smiled again. "It's really not so bad as jobs go. I can write wherever my typewriter is. That's the good part. That's why I've been able to stay down here for this long."

I pushed the heel of my sneaker down hard in the grass and turned over a wedge of red dirt. You could smell it, like the creek water. "What's dirt made out of?" I said.

"Dirt?" He reached over and picked some up. "Well, when you ask about dirt, you're asking about everything in the whole wide world, think about that. Because that's what dirt is. Animal, vegetable, mineral. It's everything, right here in my hand."

I looked at his big hand with the palm stretched open. There was the curved scar, my teeth marks, imprinted.

"I've missed this red dirt," he said, "along with a lot of other things over the past few years." He looked at me. His face was serious. "I'm hoping to stay down here, Mia. I'm hoping I'll be welcome."

I stared at my tablet, flipping through the pages. "I've been trying and trying to start this poem. I can't even start it. I can't think of the title!"

There was silence. You could just hear the trickle of the water.

"Huh," Morse Cooper said finally. "Well. Maybe you shouldn't start with a title then. Start someplace else. The title will come. It will come once you've figured out what you're writing about."

"But it does come first. I have to put it first," I said. To my surprise, I was crying. Tears were sliding onto the yellow paper. "I have to put the title first. You don't know. You only write about condiments. You don't even know!"

"Maybe I don't know," he said mildly. "But I do know this: You'll figure out your poem when you want to. I've seen something of your determination, Mia. You know, you remind me of your mom that way, going after what you want."

I put my hands over my ears. Tears were running down my cheeks. "How can I write any poem if you're just here talking and talking!"

He started to say something more, but I kept my hands pressed against my ears. Finally he gave up. He got up from the ground and brushed the grass off his khaki shorts.

I watched miserably from under my ragged bangs. He shouldn't go. I wanted him to tell me more. I wanted him to stay.

He looked down at me. I shut my eyes. When I opened

them, I saw the back of his head, his white shirt. He was going the wrong way, back along the path where the thorns would claw his skin. I could have told him, but I didn't. It was his own fault. It just was.

I went to Mrs. Swope's house, carrying a bouquet of chicory and black-eyed Susans from the vacant lot. I hadn't seen her for a while since I'd been spending my time downtown, with the Devotions. Now I had a plan, though. I hoped to come live with her. I had just thought of it. It would solve everything. I wouldn't have to give up the creek or the woods or the vacant lot, but I would be free from those evenings at the dinner table and how they all looked at me with anxious eyes, wanting something. I would be free from them.

I rang Mrs. Swope's bell.

When she arrived to unlatch the screen, I couldn't think what to say. I thrust forward the bunch of flowers and said, "Here."

"Well, bless your heart. Come on in." She pushed open the screen, and I stepped into the front hall. My new home. I had been here often, but now I looked at it differently. I followed Mrs. Swope straight back to the kitchen, taking new note of things: the small rocking chair, just my size; the baby blue Princess telephone, far superior to Kit's standard black model; the cigar box on the kitchen counter that held glue, tape, rubber bands, and pens, everything I would need for mending my paper dolls. This was going to work out.

"Well," Mrs. Swope said, "I guess you've been right busy. I feel like you grew an inch or two since I saw you last." She was putting the flowers I'd brought into a glass of water. The room smelled like buttered toast. I was impatient to ask her, but I thought I shouldn't blurt it out.

"Do you have any jobs you want done?" I said. "Because I could help you out. I'd be happy to help. For free."

"Well, bless your heart, what a good girl. I'm sure there is something. I feel like I get farther behind in my chores every minute, I'm so slow now. Let me just think."

"How about the spare bedroom? I could clean out all those boxes of papers and things that are piled up in there. In case you needed to use it."

"Oh, honey, those are Buddy's things. His school reports and such. All his mementos. Someday he's going to come back to collect them." She picked up the flowers. "Now, here's something you can do. Carry these pretty things in yonder and set them on the coffee table."

I did it, sighing. Things never just worked out easily, the way I wanted them to. In the living room I scowled at the framed photographs of Buddy's la-di-da baton-twirler daughters. I poked through the stack of magazines on the table. A subscription to *Life* and to *Field and Stream*. That would be good at least. At the far end of the room was a low bookcase jammed with books. I went over and knelt in front of it, to see what poems she had.

Mrs. Swope stepped in through the doorway, drying her hands with a dish towel. "There you are," she said. "Just kneeling before the books! Well, Kit told me you're quite a reader."

"But this is all *bird* books."

"That's right. That's most of what we have. Oh, Wishart read everything on birds that he could find. You know we were bird-watchers, the both of us. I just haven't kept up with it since he's been gone."

"Maybe you should get some new books then. Different types."

"Oh, no, thank you. I don't need to take up new things at my age. But, honey, I'll tell you, we had us some fun tracking down the birds all those years. We went hither and yon. Everybody knew Wishart."

"Huh," I said. My knees hurt, so I stood up. "Do you have any iced tea? I love that iced tea you make."

We took glasses outside to the front porch and sat in wooden chairs. I sipped my tea. She put orange juice in and other things, spices, that made it so good. If I lived here, I would drink it every day.

"Back in 1933 they wrote Wishart up for the newspaper," Mrs. Swope was saying. "They were voting on the official Tennessee state bird then, and he led the campaign for the bobwhite."

Straight across the street was Kit's brown house, flanked by the massive catalpas. Where I used to live, I told myself. Where I once lived for a while. Bibi and Nell were out on the porch swing. You could just see their sandaled feet.

"Oh, Wishart worked so hard! He wrote letters and sent them out to the whole membership of the Ornithological Society at his own expense. Of course, then the mockingbird won, and he was crushed. He never much liked that whole group of birds—the Mimidae. He thought they were show-offy. But he never spoke out. He wasn't that type. When a vote is taken, you put aside your own feelings and honor it. That's how he always did."

I watched Bibi stand up and stretch. She dropped one hand to the back of her neck. Even from here I knew what she was doing, twisting a piece of her dark gold hair around her finger until it snarled, her bad habit. I knew what she would do next: go into the house for a hairbrush. She opened the screen door and went in.

"Anyhow, we traveled," Mrs. Swope said. "We went clear up to Canada just to see a harlequin duck one time. And we took trips to Florida purely on account of the Bahama swallow or the mangrove cuckoo."

"The *cuckoo?*" I said. Now she had my attention. "That one that flies off and leaves its baby? I wouldn't go two miles to look at that bird. I wouldn't go two feet."

Mrs. Swope set her empty glass on the small table next to us. "Well, honey, you're mixing up two different birds. The one you're talking about is the true cuckoo that I've never seen. But Wishart saw them in France during the war. He said they had the prettiest call. Two notes, but not like a cuckoo clock. Not what you'd expect. It's two notes that make you want to go with them, just follow them wherever."

"Not me. I wouldn't." I set my glass down, hard, on the table. The air on the porch was so hot and still I couldn't believe that things would really change, that fall would come soon, followed by a winter. "I would shoot that bird if I found it. For what it does. I would."

"Naw, I wouldn't blame that bird, honey. I don't think it has a choice. I think it just looks out at the big blue sky and it has to go. It has to fly. Can you understand that?"

"No," I said, but for a surprising instant I did understand. I felt it. Staring sullenly out at the road, at the line of boxy houses, trying to pull the thick, hot air into your lungs. How it would be, that irresistible rush of wings, lifting you up, carrying you away. But no, I took a deep breath and my chest shuddered. I was safe, just now, just here, smelling the muddy creek water from down the road.

"Also, the mama cuckoo doesn't fly off leaving her baby in just any nest," Mrs. Swope continued. "She picks the right one. It's for a purpose."

"What?" I said. "What *purpose?*"

Mrs. Swope removed her glasses and wiped them on the hem of her dress. "To stir things up probably." She put her glasses back on and peered at me. "Because, oh, the trouble that cuckoo's child makes for the nest. Shoving and pecking at all the others, trying to rule the roost. It's a wonder anybody will take it in."

I sat still in my chair. I could feel the wooden slats pressing my skin. I thought I could feel all my separate bones pressing back. "But somebody has to take it," I said. "It can't be all alone!"

"No, it can't," Mrs. Swope agreed. "That's what it has to learn."

"Well, maybe it can't help acting that way. Maybe something makes it just act that way."

"That's what I'm saying." Mrs. Swope stood up. "Birds do what they have to do. It's instinct. My guess is that the cuckoo's child gets put in a nest where they need its kind of trouble. The nest where it should stay."

She picked up the empty tea glasses. "Enough bird talk now. Next time you'll know better than to get me started. I ought to go in and fix my dinner. Anyhow, they'll be looking for you over yonder, honey. You know, they'll be wanting you home."

CHAPTER

23

In Beirut sometimes I would hide things. Her black evening bag. Her topaz earrings. Anything, just to keep her. I put them in the broom closet or the wastebasket, and then I helped her search in the likelier places: under her bed, behind her bureau. Together we tugged the bureau away from the wall. I stood so close I could smell her lipstick. I could feel the heat of her skin. That was what I dreamed now, that warmth, the sweet red lipstick.

"Mia?"

I opened my eyes. It was only Kit, sitting next to my bed, biting her lip, already chewing her lipstick off. "We're going," she said. "I thought I'd better get you up before we go. Morse is taking me over now to get my casts cut off."

The sunlight was coming in, striped, through the slats of the blinds. I shut my eyes again. The way it turned out was that they would always go. She could choose another pair of earrings and decide not to bother with a purse, just slip her comb and her compact into my dad's pocket. It was that simple. They would always go.

"It's funny," Kit said. "Thinking about these casts. I don't know. It's just that, well, we've been through a lot, the two of us. Haven't we? Mia? Are you awake?"

She reached down and touched my head. I batted her hand away. I didn't want to wake up. I'd just remembered. It was the last day of Bible School. I was supposed to wear a dress.

"Okay. Fine." Kit stood up. "Be that way, Mia. Just push me away. I'm getting used to it anyway."

"Oh, boo-hoo," I said.

She turned and walked to the door, swinging her arms in their fiery red casts.

"Yeah," I called after her, "better get those casts cut off so you can hold Morse Cooper tight. So you can kissy kissy. I know what you do. I know!"

The door slammed. I lay there, not moving. In a while I heard the car engine start and the crunch of gravel as it backed out of the driveway. I heard Bibi and Nell talking and banging dishes around in the kitchen. I stared at the pine knots on the wall until I was tired of lying there, tired of my whole room. I got up and opened the door that led to the kitchen. My sisters were dressed and sitting at the table.

"How come you're up so early?" I said.

"We're going over to register at the high school," Nell said.

"I thought you said you would never go to school here in a million years. You said you would rather just go to jail if the truant officer came to get you."

"Yeah, well, you know, there comes a time to face facts, Mia, and to make the best of what you've got."

"Is that what you're wearing to the high school? Those black clothes?"

"Oh, God," Bibi said, "I can't stand it. Now we get a fashion critique. Let's go, Nell. Let's get there in time to sign up for the advanced classes."

"If there are any." Nell swallowed the last of her coffee and got up from the table.

"At least don't put on shawls," I said. "I mean, you don't need them here. It's hot. You don't see people wearing shawls." I remembered my own wardrobe problems then. How would I get a dress? No matter what, I couldn't unlatch the suitcase that was in the back of my closet with all of my skirts and dresses inside. I couldn't disobey what I had obeyed all summer long. "Wait," I called to my sisters. "Do you have a dress I could wear? I need a dress."

"Oh, sure," Nell said. "First you insult our clothes, then you want to borrow them. That's rich."

"Come on. Just *one* dress! You have a ton of them." I felt desperate. Three different members of the Devotions had telephoned the night before to make sure I knew Corinne's instructions. Dresses. And good shoes.

"You have plenty of them, too, Mia. Anyhow, think about it: You'd look pretty ridiculous in our clothes."

"Oh, yeah? Well, you look ridiculous in them, too! Everybody thinks so. They laugh at you when you walk down the street here."

"What?" Bibi's white face went whiter. "Who does?"

"Who cares? Don't even listen to her," Nell said. "We don't care." But her face looked stricken, too, behind her big glasses. "You know, it's just this town, Bibi. And anyway, she's only saying that because she didn't get what she wants. She's probably making it up. Let's just go now. Let's go on to the high school and get it over with."

They walked out, leaving me there alone.

I raced to the front door and pressed my face to the screen. "I didn't make it up. They said you looked like Martians!" I shouted.

Bibi and Nell didn't turn around. Their posture was stiff and dignified. Their sandals flapped.

"Martians!" I screamed at their straight backs. "From Mars!"

I sank down, miserably, onto the straw doormat, burying my head in my hands. Nothing ever worked out. Nobody cared. I just got meaner and meaner. And I still didn't have a dress.

At Bible School Mrs. Wilmott gave us each a gilded white leather bookmark to remember her by. Her eyes were damp. Now she and Mr. Wilmott would return to their college studies in Nashville, she told us. They would move back into the basement apartment where Mr. Wilmott's parents generously let them live, rent-free, for the winter. On the other side of the basement Mr. Wilmott's father kept something she'd bet we would like to see. More than a dozen cages of furry little chinchillas. They had big dark eyes, and they appeared so calm and still in the daytime, just twitching their ears, you would never guess that, every night, all night, they liked to thump their legs against the bars and gnaw on the newspaper that lined their cages. You could hear them right through the partition walls.

"Those rascals. Such energy. Chewing. Chewing. All night long. Chomp. Chomp. Chomp. Chomp. Chomp." Mrs. Wilmott smiled, wringing her large hands. "Imagine."

We practiced the hymns we would sing later in a show for all the parents. Then there would be punch and cookies served. Earlier in the week they had given out dittoed invitations for us to take home. I loved the smell of the purple ink. I had sniffed my invitation for half the walk home. Then I stuffed it down a storm drain.

At the end of the streets the storm drains emptied into the creeks. The creeks flowed into the river. The river led down to the sea. I thought of all that. I thought of them, how they could fish the invitation out of the sea and decide to sail home, to hear me sing.

I touched my dress now, smoothing the pleated skirt. Things had worked out surprisingly well after all. When my sisters went around the corner, out of sight, I got up off the doormat and ransacked all the closets, pulling things off hangers and out of dry cleaner bags. In the cedar closet, off the back hallway, I found it. A royal blue dress with a pleated skirt, short enough to fit me. It was plain and baggy on the top, but it did fit. And it had the added feature of matching bloomers attached. If you climbed something, nobody could see your underwear. All dresses should come that way. My black patent leather shoes were tight, but I had managed to stuff my feet in. I was all set.

Mrs. Wilmott dismissed us, dabbing her eyes with a Kleenex. Some of the little girls flocked around her, patting her arms, being nice. I hobbled off to the girls' room in my shiny, painful shoes. I wondered where Sinclair was. She had not been standing in her assigned place on the wooden risers when we practiced our singing. In the girls' room only Lady-Anne was there, already in front of a sink, brushing her teeth. I admired my reflection. Blue was a good color on me. I undid the top snap of the dress, but there was my knobby collarbone. I snapped it back up.

Lady-Anne leaned over and spit hard into the sink. Some splattered back on her shirt, but she didn't notice. You couldn't do anything; you couldn't help her. There was too much she didn't know.

"Lady-Anne," I said, "have you seen Sinclair around?"

"No." She tapped her toothbrush on the rim of the sink to get the water out. "Not since she quit."

"She *quit?* What? She quit Bible School? Why would she quit Bible School now?"

"Well, she quit two days ago." Lady-Anne shrugged her droopy little shoulders. "She said she had better things to do."

Better things. There it was again. But what things? What could she be up to now? Without me. I had to find out. I wasn't going to get left behind. *Better things.* It gave me a feeling like an itch.

"I have a question," Lady-Anne said. "How come you're wearing that gym suit?"

"What?" My hands flew up to the blue neckline. "This? It's not—" I spun away, toward the mirror. The snaps. The bloomers. It was. Of course, it was. I stood there, reflected, a shocked-looking girl in a gym suit.

"It's what they wear for gym at Ionia High School," Lady-Anne said. "Everybody knows that. It's the kind they've had for years and years. My mama has an old one just like that. She puts it on when the person from the beauty shop comes to wax her legs. It's more modest than putting on just a bathing suit. My mama says people shouldn't—"

I turned and left the rest room, sprinting as quickly as I could on my tortured feet. Outside I blinked in the brightness. The sky was brilliant. I had dressed myself in Kit's old gym suit from the cedar closet. I reached down and pulled off my shoes so I could get away, fast, before the Devotions came. But, already it was too late. They were on the path, heading this way, a tight clutch of pastel colors and white shoes. Nobody told me *white* shoes. Nobody ever said that.

I crawled around behind the oak tree, jumped up and caught the lowest branch. I could still climb. I was always good at climbing.

"Mia, what are you doing?" It was Ellen's voice below me. I looked down and there they all were, in a flock, beneath the tree, staring up.

"Climbing," I answered. "I'm climbing." I went higher and sat on the crook of a branch to rub my throbbing toes.

"Mia, Corinne says for you to come down right now."

"No, I won't."

They all breathed in, startled. I swung my bare feet. Suddenly, everything felt turned around. I had the power. They couldn't come up here in their crinoline dresses. They couldn't touch me. And I didn't need them after all. I could do what I wanted. I could dress how I wanted. I could climb.

"She's going higher!"

"Somebody make her get *down*."

Corinne took a step forward. The others backed out of her way. She looked up at me with her narrowed, satisfied eyes. I saw then: this was a moment she'd been planning for. "Go on," she said. "Climb as high as you want. We don't care. We were just letting you hang around with us, but that's over with now."

"I know," I said. I felt light, as if wings could lift me, the way I'd felt for that moment on Mrs. Swope's porch.

I looked down at their upturned faces, the battalion of matching white shoes. Oh, they could never fly; they couldn't even guess.

"Corinne, I think we should go," somebody said. "It's time to go sing."

Through the leaves I could see the parents beginning to file in and find seats in the folding chairs that had been set up across the parking lot. The dads had the cameras on straps around their necks, the moms pulled themselves tall in their seats, looking past all the others, looking for their own child.

"I know, let's go," Corinne agreed. "She can just stay up there alone, a nut in a tree." She turned and they all followed her back along the path.

"I'm not alone," I said into the still air. "I'm waiting for somebody."

When the singing began, I sang, too, up in the tree. I sang, just waiting, my legs dangling from the branch. I sang until the singing was all over and the chairs scraped on the blacktop as everybody stood up.

Then they were eating and talking, and what you heard most was the low rumble of the dads' voices. It could make you shiver. The kids posed for pictures, and before the camera clicked, the mom would lick her thumb and lean down to rub a punch stain off a chin. The kid would twist back, pulling away from her, as if she'd always be right there. Okay, smile! the dad would say, and the kid clowned around, making faces, going cross-eyed, but I did it. I smiled, ready, in the tree.

People started calling out good-byes and getting into their cars. A crew of men pulled the risers apart. They folded the chairs and tables and carried everything into the basement. After they left, it was so quiet you could hear the locusts nibbling on the bushes. I sat there, the ridges of bark pressing into my skin. The sun went lower and the church made a tilted shadow, a parallelogram, on the grass. I watched the shadow drift across the lawn until it was out of sight. Just like that, you saw how the world kept moving. No matter what you did to hold it, it moved on.

"See, I can't wait anymore," I whispered to the deepening sky. "I've waited as hard as I could."

I slid over toward the tree trunk, looking for a way back down.

Stop! I heard the order. *Stay in the tree.*

But I wouldn't. The power was just gone. All summer I let myself believe it, but now I couldn't. I wasn't a saint. I was just a kid in a gym suit, up a tree, all alone. Now I wanted to come down.

A car pulled into the parking lot, fast, the beam of its headlights slashing over the grass. A door slammed, and my aunt cried out, "Mia? Mee-yahh!"

She ran across the blacktop, around the building, and then up the path, right below the tree. "Mee-yah!"

"Here," I said. She froze. "I'm here, Kit. I'm in the tree."

She looked up and burst into tears.

"It's okay," I told her. "I'm coming down."

"Nothing—hear me?—*nothing* has made me this upset in twenty years," Kit sobbed. "But you've done it, Mia. God! You've got everybody going. Morse is down at the creek, looking for you. Bibi and Nell are walking over here, calling your name at every street corner along the way. You can't do this, I'm telling you, Mia. You can't just run away from us!"

"Well." I took a breath. "I wasn't—"

"It isn't just *you*, Mia," Kit interrupted. "You're not the only one! She left me behind, too, all those years ago, and it broke my heart, how much I missed her. My big sister. And Morse, she left Morse after that. All of us. Don't you think we're all in this together?"

"I don't know," I said, looking out at the night. "It feels like just me."

"Oh, honey," Kit said.

I stabbed the black air, blindly, with my toes, feeling for the next branch. Then I was dropping, skidding down the trunk, scraping my shin, finally landing on the bottom limb, just above my aunt's head.

"Mia!" She screamed.

"I'm okay." My heart thudded from the thrill of falling.

"See, you jump out of *trees*!" She was crying again. "And off water towers! What am I supposed to do with you? You already broke both my arms. This is the first time I've been without casts in weeks and weeks, and here you are climbing again. You saw to it that Dan Flannery was out of my life. And now you're working on driving Morse away, too, aren't you? You're so rude to him. You won't look him in the eye. You won't even speak his name."

"Are you going to marry him?"

"Oh, God, Mia, who knows? Who knows? Things aren't ever just that simple. That's what you have to learn. I've learned it, all right, ever since you got here. God, nothing's simple now!"

"Because," I said, "if you marry him, what would you be—Bibi and Nell's stepmother or their aunt?"

"Mia, *please*. Come down here and we'll talk about everything."

"And you all would be named Cooper then, wouldn't you? But not me. I would be Veery."

"Well," Kit said, "that's what I was telling you. Things aren't simple, especially families. Families are full of complications."

"Maybe I should just go someplace else." I dabbed my finger at the beads of blood on my scraped shin. "Maybe I could go live at that county home."

"Oh, you make me just furious!" Kit said. "Don't you listen to anything? What do you think I'm doing standing out in the dark talking you down from a tree? I could never go back to how it was before you came, don't you know that? Oh, you just drive me crazy! Mia, don't you see? I could never, ever let you go."

My sisters burst in through the gate of the parking lot, waving a flashlight and hollering my name.

"Here," Kit called to them. "She's here."

They raced in our direction, zigzagging the flashlight until the beam caught me there in the tree.

"There she is," Nell said.

"Oh, thank God," Bibi said.

"I thought you didn't believe in God," I said. "Anyhow, get that light out of my face. I can't see."

"Mia," Nell said. "Oh, Mia, everything's going to be okay. I mean, we're all here together, Mia. Just don't run away anymore."

Another car skidded into the parking lot. "Hello? Hello? Kit? I couldn't find her. She wasn't anywhere at the creek."

"She's here, Morse! We're all over here."

"And she's okay," Nell called. "She's just up in a tree."

"Nell," Bibi said in a wondering voice. "Look. She's wearing a *gym suit*. Like the ones they handed out at the high school today."

"You're right," Nell said. "She really is. That's rich. The one for whom appearance is everything runs away from home wearing nothing but a gym suit."

I slid down, out of the tree, escaping the beam of light. I wanted to go, to just get away from all of them. I took a step and fell down. My legs were asleep after sitting so long.

Morse Cooper reached down and set me carefully back on my feet.

"Thank you," I said. "Morse."

I brushed myself off. My legs felt useless, stuck with

ten thousand pins. Anyway, there was nowhere left to go. They knew about the creek. They would find me. Always they would find me. I sighed. "Number one," I said to all of them, "I do not care about appearances. Maybe I did, but now I don't. So, anybody can just wear what they want and nobody needs to say anything. Number two, I was *not* running away from home."

"Well, what *were* you doing then? Why were you up in the tree?"

"I was waiting."

"For what?"

My mouth shook. "Everybody else's family came. I wanted mine, too."

"But how were we supposed to know?" Kit said. "How were we supposed to come here if nobody told us?"

I blinked, looking at them, their four tall shapes, standing close, the only thing between me and the endless dark sky. "I don't know," I said. "But here you are."

My aunt stepped forward and swooped me into her mended arms. I knew just what I was saying. At last I was saying yes.

CHAPTER

24

For three days I tried to reach Sinclair on the telephone, but she was never home. I left messages for her to call me back, but she didn't. I decided I would have to go to her house and track her down.

When I got there, I almost lost my nerve. I hid in the pepperbushes out front and stared across the lawn at the wide brick house. It looked even more imposing than I remembered. Its upstairs windows were like eyes, judging me, how I'd treated Sinclair. I took a step back out onto the sidewalk, and I was nearly run over by Sinclair herself, hurtling along on a boy's English bike. She swerved around me, scraping her shoes on the pavement to slow down. Then she leaped off, letting the bike crash on its side in the grass.

"It doesn't have a kickstand," she said, breathlessly, "or

brakes. It used to be my brother's, and he disconnected everything. Only one gear works."

"Maybe you need a new bike," I said.

"Oh, I have a new one," Sinclair said dismissively. She carried a gray knapsack, strapped over one shoulder. Her hair stuck straight up in the front after her ride, like a cockatoo's crest. "Anyhow, what were you doing, spying on my house?"

"Sinclair." My voice wavered. "I came to apologize. I'm truly, truly sorry. Can we be friends again?"

She eyed me. "That doesn't sound convincing," she said finally. "It sounds like something on a greeting card."

I balled up my fists: then I let them drop. I never hit people. Usually I didn't even want to hit people. What I really wanted now was to go inside and sit on the blue rug and make plans for how to go on. I wanted everything to start again. "I've been calling you for three days," I said.

"Yeah, well, I've been busy. Sketching."

"Sketching?"

"Um-hmm. I'm an artist now. I sketch things. That's where I've just been." She waved one hand, vaguely. "Out. Sketching."

"Oh. Could I see? What you've been drawing."

She turned her inky eyes on me. "Why? Don't you believe me?"

Then I didn't. "Why?" I said back. "Where have you *really* been?"

"Oh, I knew it! You did come over here to spy on me, didn't you? To tell the little cheerleaders all about it."

They would never care a bit what Sinclair might be doing, but I didn't say that. I shifted my weight from one leg to the other on the hard sidewalk. "It's just me, Sinclair. It's not them. They're nothing now."

"Well, how do I know that? How do I know you won't just go and join up with them again?"

I thought of the answer. The words terrified me. It was choosing the shape of your whole life. I said it: "I can't go back. I tried it, and now I know. Sinclair, I can't be just regular."

Her hurt, wary face loosened. She leaned toward me. "Okay," she said in a confiding voice. "I'll tell you. There's this boy. I've been meeting this boy. We've kissed six times."

"Sinclair!" I looked at her. She seemed the same, her cockatoo hair, her sleepy posture, but she wasn't. She was so far ahead of me now. I didn't know what I would do if she just went on, leaving me behind.

"There's muscles in your lips," she said. "Did you ever think of that? Especially if you use them a lot, like if you play an instrument." She looked at me. "He plays the slide trombone."

I couldn't stand it. Everything. The low thrill of the word *trombone*. "Sinclair," I said, "do you think maybe he knows somebody else? You know, somebody for me?"

"I guess," she said. "Sure, probably. Eugene has lots of friends."

"It's *Eugene?* That one from Bible School? You told me he liked me. You said he was looking at me all the time."

"I was wrong," Sinclair shrugged. "He was looking at me." She picked up the bike and started wheeling it across the lawn. "Well, come on in, little spy," she said. "Let's get something to eat."

I followed her across the grass. A boy would kiss me, soon. I wished I had my tablet of yellow paper with me. I had been writing things down: the shape of my dad's hands; my mom's smile; how her eyes changed color like the light on the sea in Beirut. I couldn't keep them, but I wouldn't ever let them go. Oh, they had tried to tell me everything in the world, and I never paid good attention, but now I was. Now I was ready to write down new things, ready for what came next.

We sat on the blue rug and ate raisin cookies, the flat kind that you separate, along dotted lines, like postage stamps.

"I'm going to sketch you," Sinclair said. "Right now." She unbuckled the gray knapsack and took out a sketchbook. "See? I wasn't lying before. I really am an artist. I have charcoal pencils, too."

I swallowed my cookie. She couldn't get ahead of me again. "Well, I'm a poet. I'm already writing a poem, or it might be a whole book of poems." I paused. "And it has a title: 'The Cuckoo's Child.' " It had come to me just now, sitting right here.

" 'The Cuckoo's Child,' " Sinclair repeated. She held a black pencil, point up, in the air. " 'Stand still, true poet that you are!' " She smiled her wide, drowsy smile. "I didn't make that up. It's part of a poem. I only know poems by Browning. That's what my dad reads to us."

"Well, I can tell you some by Edna St. Vincent Millay. She's the best."

"And the best artist is Picasso," Sinclair said. "I'll show you in a book. He does these crazy paintings because he's a cubic."

I smiled down at the rug. She might be ahead of me, but I knew she had the wrong word. And I knew the right one. It was something they all discussed again and again at our dinner table. I was finally paying attention.

"Cuban." I corrected her gently. "It's an island next to Russia."

Sinclair's pencil scratched boldly over the paper. I lifted my arms out, stretching. The room was so big, but already it felt too tiny to hold us, with all that we knew, everything we were ready to take on.

And wherever they might be, oh, they could be proud of me now.